3—

MON AMIE AMÉRICAINE

ALSO BY MICHÈLE HALBERSTADT

The Pianist in the Dark
La Petite

MON AMIE AMÉRICAINE

Michèle Halberstadt

TRANSLATED FROM THE FRENCH BY

Bruce Benderson

OTHER PRESS
NEW YORK

"Comic Strip" lyrics on page 14 by Serge Gainsbourg, from the album *Bonnie and Clyde*, 1968. Translated from the French by Bill Solly.

Production editor: Yvonne E. Cárdenas
Text designer: Julie Fry
This book was set in Fournier and Neutra
by Alpha Design & Composition of Pittsfield, NH

10 9 8 7 6 5 4 3 2 1

Library of Congress Cataloging-in-Publication Data

Names: Halberstadt, Michèle. | Benderson, Bruce, translator.
Title: Mon amie américaine / Michèle Halberstadt ; translated from the
    French by Bruce Benderson.
Other titles: Mon amie américaine. English
Description: New York : Other Press, 2016.
Identifiers: LCCN 2015031208| ISBN 9781590517598 (paperback) | ISBN
    9781590517604 (e-book)
Subjects: LCSH: Female friendship—Fiction. | BISAC: FICTION /
    Contemporary Women. | FICTION / Literary. | FICTION /
    Psychological.
Classification: LCC PQ2668.A3637 M6613 2016 | DDC 843/.914—dc23 LC
    record available at http://lccn.loc.gov/2015031208

For Arthur, my son

If the sky above you
Grows dark and full of clouds
And that old north wind begins to blow
Keep your head together
And call my name out loud
Soon you'll hear me knocking at your door.

— CAROLE KING, "YOU'VE GOT A FRIEND"

I HAD GONE DOWN TO BUY SOME HONEY COUGH DROPS. There was a ticklish feeling in my throat and my nose was stuffed, the beginnings of a cold. It was ten p.m. and the drugstore was about to close. In the distance, a dance of cranes signaled the putting up of Christmas decorations on the Champs-Elysées, decking out the plane trees with white tulle, which made them look like gigantic candies.

I took the six flights back upstairs on foot to get some air into my lungs and clear out the cold. By the time I'd turned the key in the lock and pushed open the door, Vincent was coming toward me with a rueful look I'd never known before. I'd seen him defeated, depressed — but this was different. It was me he was sorry for, like a doctor with bad news he wished he didn't have to announce.

Instantly I thought of you, so intensely that I said aloud what was already no longer a question but a fact: "Molly."

His head nodded so sadly that it seemed to move in slow motion. "She's in a coma."

I raised a hand to interrupt him.

I didn't want an explanation. I didn't want to hear anything, understand anything, discuss anything. I opened the door to the bedroom and carefully closed it behind me.

Alone. I needed to be alone to face the din roaring in my head. It was as if a thousand people had connected to my brain to scramble its data and keep me from thinking.

I sat down in an armchair without turning on the light. A red button was blinking noiselessly on the keys of the telephone. The darkness gave it a scarlet tinge I thought was appropriate, since red was the color of a scream, emergency, fear. The blood in my veins was like an immense wave that had invaded everything and suddenly pulled away. I'd been so warm, and suddenly I felt frozen. My heart was beating to the rhythm of the gleam, which was still blinking imperturbably, giddily, like a flashing ambulance light with the siren cut off.

Images of you passed before my eyes. Dancing with our eyes shut while singing Tina Turner in your kitchen. Trying on every single pair of sunglasses at a shop in the Gare de Lyon without buying any. Disguised as a blonde for a costume party. Wolfing down a hot dog on a London street last week. At the airport, five days ago, buying a carton of cigarettes. Your willowy figure dragging the too heavy suitcase you hadn't wanted to check. Your violet-scented perfume when you kissed me goodbye. Your smile when you came back to shout to me, "Bon voyage!" Your voice hoarse, mocking, inimitable.

I didn't know I could produce so many tears.

MOLLY, I HAVE TO TALK TO YOU. Even if you can't hear me. The words I can't share with you are choking me. So I'll write to you. Not to record my actions, but to tell you what's happening during the undetermined length of your absence. Try to understand how differently we both live. I'm going to try to find the words.

I'm not going to lay them down on paper, as they say. It's a lovely expression, but it's much too gentle. No, I'm banging out my words. My two index fingers dart over the keyboard vehemently. I type the way I am: like an amateur, too fast, too hard, and often hitting the wrong key. Impetuously, imprecisely, like a beginner, everything I hate about myself. The opposite of you, always levelheaded, organized. You type like a girl Friday in the movies, at top speed, a butt hanging from your mouth casually, without ever looking at your hands, nonchalantly tinkling out your ten-finger ballet.

You've never written me. You'd rather call.

It's two p.m. where you are, in New York. In your office, you just had a bagel with smoked salmon, and you're about to tear into your second pack of menthol cigarettes for the day. But first you dialed my number and, after a few minutes of conversation, I hear you remove the cellophane and slip the cigarette between your lips. It distorts your voice long enough for the first puff, which you inhale as if exulting, with delight.

Now I know that you'll be able to concentrate on what I'm telling you. Or else you're the one who spoke first, then paused, after saying what was on your mind, before you flicked your lighter.

You used to say you'd stop smoking when you found a man to give you children, since a pregnancy was, you'd maintain, the only way to make yourself give up your three packs a day.

You didn't know that illness was another way to achieve abstinence.

There are no smoking sections in intensive care.

In German, *Komma* is pronounced almost the same way *coma* is in French, but it's spelled differently and means something else. A *Komma* is a comma in German. A pause between two words. In your case, between two territories: sleeping and waking. Rest, Molly, as long as you want. Provided you wake up.

If you knew how much I resent you! How many times in the last ten years have I repeated you ought to see a specialist, instead of "doing the ostrich." I had a hard time explaining to you what that expression — *faire l'autruche* — means in French: it means the same as *bury your head in the sand* in English. And you really got a kick out of that. A few months later, you brought me back some sand from a beach in Bahia and had written with a blue marker on the plastic bottle you'd filled: OPEN. MY HEAD'S INSIDE.

On your planet "Comma," there's neither sand nor pebbles. Only your consciousness, which it's your job to bring back intact.

Strange how you can tell yourself stories to avoid facing reality. A long weekend without being able to reach you. It didn't feel normal. I said to myself, We just came back from London, tired and jet-lagged, and she must be up to her ears in work. As if that had ever kept you from sending some news, leaving a message, answering mine. There was a holiday that Monday in the United States. During those few days I figured that you'd had to leave. As if you'd take a vacation out of the blue — you, who always plan them because you hate improvising.

I tried to reach your partners. Couldn't. Only reached their secretary's voice mail. Nobody called me back. As for Tom, he's only been your assistant for a few months, and I don't know him. I didn't have the nerve to leave him a message.

The morning of the day you lost consciousness, I was in the bathroom and I heard your horoscope on the radio: "Taurus, today you'll need the love of the people close to you." Stupidly I took that for a good omen.

IT'S SATURDAY AFTERNOON, AND THE WEATHER'S HORRIBLE. So much the better. It matches the way I feel. I burst into tears in the kitchen a little while ago. The radio was playing a French oldie, "C'est la fête," and its exuberant cheerfulness grabbed me as only a song can do. A feeling coming from far away, from the deepest reaches of my memory, and going directly to my heart. I was standing in front of the window making tea. That snatch of music pulled the ground out from under me.

In a flash I was sitting down, and the children, who were having their after-school snack, got scared and tumbled into my arms. They'd never seen me cry. What can I say to them?

Clara runs to get the giant kangaroo you gave her. It's her favorite stuffed animal. The thing is so tall that she's been curling up in it for a long time. Benoît gets miffed because he doesn't know who we're talking about, so I show him a photo of you. In it you're trying to keep on a straw hat that might have flown away an instant later. You're in a garden, it's sunny, and you're talking to someone who can't be seen, the photographer perhaps. He's managed to immortalize that pout of yours that always comes before a smile. Benoît studies you intensely. He says you're good-looking and adds, "She looks nice, why is she making you cry?" I explain to him that you're lying in a hospital bed, that I don't understand very well why and that you're sleeping so deeply that you don't hear anyone who speaks to you. Clara looks hard at me, as if she has guessed everything that I'm not saying, while Benoît smiles, because the reason seems so obvious to him. "She's waiting for Prince Charming to come and give her a kiss!" I answer that in real life it's sometimes complicated to awaken a princess. He shrugs. "Then you need to lend her your alarm clock."

If only he were right! I'd set off all the sirens in Manhattan if they could bring you back to life. Not to mention the firemen's here in Paris, which go off at noon on the dot the first Wednesday of every month. When I was little, I was convinced that there was a hidden message in that signal. So much noise couldn't be used only to indicate the day and the hour. It was a message in code, and I was willing to stake my life on it. Maybe it was signaling the beginning of the end of the world? Why wasn't anyone paying attention to it? I'd get so frightened that I'd bite the inside of my lips to the point of drawing blood. Then, as if by miracle, the ringing would stop; but I'd keep scanning the sky to spot the moment when it would become night in broad daylight. Then everyone would understand that it was a signal, but it would be too late already . . .

In New York, the police car sirens are continuously vying with those of the ambulances. One of those must have taken you to the hospital. But you didn't hear it. You were already cut off from the world. Lost on planet Comma. That unknown land each of us dreads visiting one day and that you've gone off to discover alone.

I'd rather think you're away on some assignment, out covering a story; and that you can't wait to tell me about what you've found out as soon as you get back. Are there sounds, colors? Breathtaking scenery? Is it a parched desert? Vertigo, a black hole? Stark night? A long nightmare? Apparently you're knitting your brow. You couldn't be suffering. The doctors promised that. But who can be sure? How can anyone know what you're feeling?

MOLLY, SWEET MOLLY, YOU WHO ARE ENCOUNTERING THE WORST, you have to admit that you weren't really prepared for this. You, the city rat who'll startle at the slightest noise, get hysterical when an insect comes near; you, climbing onto a chair the moment you see a mouse. You, scared of the dark, heights, flying, bridges, and elevators. Shunning exercise, jogging, sports, the slightest physical exertion. You, the American who gobbles vitamins, never eating right, the confirmed frozen-food user, eating yogurt a month after the expiration date, worshipping the sun to an outrageous extent, forgetting whether you've had a tetanus shot, sucking down aspirin like it's mint candy, abusing cheesecake and chocolate milkshakes. You, doping yourself with one cappuccino or Diet Coke after another. Swearing like a sailor and whistling like a boy with two fingers in your mouth. The most sappily romantic girl I've ever met, my incorrigible opposite, whom I've always found so wonderfully unreasonable. Acknowledge that, of the two of us, you were the less equipped to experiment with what has befallen you: this loss of consciousness, this diabolical heads or tails suspended in time, during which you spin indefinitely around like a coin that fate has tossed into the air without anyone knowing on which side it will fall, or even if it will ever fall back to earth.

I imagine you hanging on to that coin as if it's a saddle, like a cartoon pinup astride the atomic bomb, hair blowing in the wind and a wily smile, totally indifferent to that countdown that tolls the knell of her mount. Tick-tock, tick-tock . . .

> Come with me, let's get together in my comic strip.
> Let's talk in bubbles, let's go BANG! and ZIP!
> Forget your troubles and go
> SHEBAM! POW! BLOP! WIZZ . . .

I know it's ridiculous, but I still prefer imagining you with Bardot's voice in the Gainsbourg song, her breasts thrust forward, lips parted, vampish and rebellious, rather than knowing you're flat on your back and mute, your arms pierced by IVs.

Do you know what I was doing while you were falling alongside your window on the eighteenth floor of your office on Madison Avenue? I was buying shoes. You, with your fifty-eight pairs. At least that was the official figure we came up with together four months ago. Since that time, there must have been a few sales and other promotions you certainly could not resist. And also, you hadn't let me include the sandals, flip-flops, espadrilles, and other beach shoes that a person usually keeps for the seashore. "Actually, those are vacation shoes, they don't count." But if I added them, we'd be getting close to the hundreds, don't you think?

A hundred pairs of shoes. You would say I didn't know how to appreciate the beauty of them because I was a "shoe killer." It's true that no matter what pair I buy, it's transformed, deformed, stretched out of shape; and in less than a week it looks worn out, kaput. But what's going to happen to yours? Did someone think of airing out the drawers in which you keep them arranged by height and category? Do shoes go downhill when their owners abandon them? Maybe that's the reason why Benoît's Prince Charming went throughout the realm with his squirrel-trimmed slipper. Because he sensed that it felt forsaken, unhappy, utterly depressed, without its faithful other half.

If I were in New York, I'd go and slip my hand into each of them. I wouldn't try that with my feet because I'm two sizes larger than you are. Then I'd lay them on their sides on tissue paper, as you do in hotel rooms to which you always carried one more suitcase than I did because of your many pairs of shoes.

You're the champion of baggage. You always have the latest when it comes to the wheels, outer coverings, always searching for something better in terms of size and ease of handling. But whatever luggage you travel with, you also have your very own gift for botching their aesthetic by rigging them out with your dreadful fuchsia-pink labels shaped like a heart, the height of bad taste. I never knew where you bought those eyesores. Never tried to find out, either. In fact, Molly, if I loved making fun of your fuchsia labels, it was especially for the pleasure of hearing you pronounce your favorite French complaint about being pestered, with an accent so thick you could cut it with a knife: *"Tu me casses les pieds."*

Maybe it was your coming move that wore you out. You were so happy about your new neighborhood, going to a better-looking building with a terrace and a doorman in a uniform. The last shopping trip we took was to choose an extendable table for your future balcony, with its view over the Hudson. You were so looking forward to the dinners you were going to have there. I'd been planning to get you an umbrella with a gas heater made to look like a streetlamp, for dining outside. You were planning on having a house-warming party in the spring.

For three months, that's all you talked about, even though you dreaded having to get it all organized. Pack away your life in boxes. Itemize everything. Sift through memories. It can make you ill. Moving means having to listen to everything you own remind you of its story. There are the things you've inherited, those you bought on a whim, those given to you by people you were intimate with — friends, or sometimes former heartthrobs.

Coming back to you all at once. Smells you remember from childhood. Certain landscapes. Places where you used to live. Intense emotions, cries, laughter. The sound track that goes with an entire section of your former life. Memories that make you reappraise the present, and that throw a light on a future that isn't always positive. What have we gained, lost, since these objects, outfits, paintings, books, music became part of our lives? How many chances to be happy, to have been, or to have failed to be? All of it reevaluated in terms of the time passed and the years acquired. Enough to make you sink into a pit of melancholy.

Well, I'm talking about me. You yourself like to foster memories; you can even say it's the way you live. You've hung photos everywhere in your two-room apartment — on the walls, the furniture, even on the door to the bathroom and on the refrigerator. The ones of your family and friends are arranged haphazardly, in a patchwork that only makes sense to you. The snapshots of those you've been working with for the last twenty years are framed and prominently displayed. The fact that they're well-known personalities doesn't bother you. The opposite, in fact.

We talked about it countless times. "For once," you'd say laughingly, "it's the French woman who's the most uptight of the two!" No doubt about that. It isn't such exposure that puts me ill at ease. Although that, too. You just don't show off your life in that way, flaunt the faces of the celebrities with whom you regularly rub shoulders. After all, our work life is no one's business but our own. You appear in each of the prints as if you were trying to immortalize that moment, the way the worst sixteen-year-old schoolgirl would. To accomplish what? For whom? For you? But you've lived that moment, it's inscribed in your memory. What makes you want to keep a tangible souvenir of it? Why do you need those photos? What do you have to prove? You'd say that your real calling was being a fan, that you'd wanted to work in film to become a professional groupie. One day you admitted to me that you'd stood in the rain for ten hours straight waiting to get Tina Turner's autograph. You put yourself in a position to get a continual and permanent high being around stars every day. You got a thrill reading fan magazines.

When a photo taken at the Oscars showed you with your arm threaded under Almodóvar's, you bought dozens of copies of the magazine. No one could even see your face . . .

I never succeeded in making you admit that there was something dubious, immature about that stuff spread all over your apartment. You'd make fun of my inability to take things lightly. You thought my embarrassment about those photos was more suspect than the pleasure you took in living surrounded by them. I'd call you Miss Desmond, like the American actress played by Gloria Swanson in *Sunset Boulevard*, who can't stand the fact that she isn't being worshipped as a silent movie star any more.

Now I feel bad about having made fun of you so often. Could it be that, down deep, you saw those shots as proof of your success? Since the work you did was your whole life? I'm thinking of your empty apartment, those photos of you, your radiant smile in each of them. All those traces of your shimmering life. Thinking of it tears at my heart.

MOLLY, YOU'VE BEEN IN A PRIVATE ROOM FOR EIGHT DAYS. I'm not sure that's a good sign. After more than a month, it's now obvious that this coma is going to last.

I know that nurses come in and massage you every morning. Is it possible that you don't feel them at all? Or are you suspended above your body? Are you watching them doing their work with surprise? Curiosity? Indifference?

You're still hooked up to your machines. On one side are the ones that help you breathe and feed you; on the other are those measuring your vital signs. No one is allowed to come near you without being dressed like an astronaut: body covered with a layer of pale blue plastic, shoes, too. Apparently, only medical equipment can be in your room. No flowers, drawings, get-well cards, objects, candles, tchotchkes. As you can imagine, I tried everything.

Around you, we're getting organized. You'd enjoy seeing your friends interacting. I don't know if you knew how jealous we were of one another. You certainly made connections all over the world. One friend from Rome, another from Berlin, a third from London; and me, the Parisian. Each of us was firmly convinced she was the closest to you. And in her own way, each of us was right. It's as if you'd divided your personality into four equal parts.

The woman from Berlin was your surrogate mother. You'd put yourself under her wing. She represented solace, the assurance of being understood without being judged. The woman from London was your neurotic twin, the head side of the coin to your tails. Bulimia belonged to her, diets to you. Both of you had the same hang-ups. The Italian woman was your exotic cousin, and you could admire her without being jealous; she's so different that it's not even possible to resent her for being beautiful, brilliant, and sophisticated. For you, an American born in Brooklyn, she was the embodiment of European culture at its most refined.

And what was I in all of that? I arrived last. You and I had the same profession, almost the same age, Jewish Ashkenazi culture, the same sense of humor, and a first name beginning with the same letter. Each of us was what the other could have been if the cards had been shuffled and dealt differently. Yes, I could have been that little girl brought up in Brooklyn by a housewife and a dentist father, inhibited by two cheekier sisters. I could have been that girl who fled the nest at seventeen to escape the narrow confines of a conventional petit-bourgeois family that respected the stifling precepts of Jewishness to the letter. I could have become a confirmed single and spent my life, like you, traveling the world, instead of starting a family.

You could have grown up in Paris in a less traditional family that was nonetheless just as taxing. You would have extended your studies a tad longer, would have a husband and children, would be living in Paris; and the pleasure of traveling for work would have been spoiled by feeling constantly guilty about deserting your family. And today, you would be feeling robbed of that other self stuck in a hospital bed. Like me, you would be feeling the frustration of not being able to speak to her or hear her. You'd be living in anxiety and waiting, in futile questioning. You'd be spending hours on medical forums trying to understand what has happened.

There's no question that you'd be more rational, less impatient than me. You would definitely have filled one of those eternal, habitual tables of yours, divided into two columns: FOR and AGAINST. You'd say that it helped you think clearly. I've always thought it was a waste of time.

This time, if only for you, I do want to try it.

The pluses: you're in the prime of life, barely forty years old; you're a fighter and I hope you stay that way, even in the coma; you're rarely sick, never tired; you've always said you had strength born of despair. Now is the time to use it.

The minuses: your coma is lasting an abnormally long time, if I can believe what I've read about that on the Internet; you used to eat anything at all and I'm positive you don't have enough red blood cells, proteins, a lot of healthy stuff. What else? You smoke too much, obviously, but that harms the lungs, not the brain, as far as I know.

Now I know what I hate about that binary way of approaching a problem: it doesn't leave any place for the irrational.

Were you born under a good star, Molly? In the midst of all this misfortune, will you have any luck?

IT STILL IS USELESS TO INSIST: only your parents and sisters have the right to visit you, just as they have for the last month and a half. I'll bet they're talking to you about personal things. They must be bringing up memories, regrets, maybe things they feel sorry for. I've never met them, but I figure they have your discretion and your reticence. I hope you're not being exposed to those maudlin scenes shown in all the American tearjerkers. Remember how we both used to snivel watching Debra Winger dying of cancer in *Terms of Endearment*? Or when Susan Sarandon, who was at death's door, forgives Julia Roberts for having snatched her husband in *Stepmom*? Molly, if you come out of this, I'll bring you the DVD collection of all the films that made us cry; but still, I'm not planning on rewatching a single one because they never end well for the character in the hospital.

I wonder how your family can stand this waiting, these hours spent in your room at your side, with you so near yet so unreachable.

You would say that in order to better love your parents, you needed to be far away from them. That when you were with them, you felt yourself regressing, becoming a little girl again. And no matter how much I'd explain to you that every adult permanently remains her parents' child, you didn't seem convinced.

You were outraged at the dinner for your parents' fiftieth anniversary a few months ago when they lectured you for having given them too expensive a present. "They've always dreamed of going on a safari in Kenya, but when I give it to them, they're obsessed with how much I paid for it. They ought to be happy that I can afford it instead of supervising what I do with my money! In my family, we're always worrying instead of enjoying." I explained to you that mine operated on the same model and that it was obvious that Holocaust survivors have a hard time putting any levity in their life, but you wouldn't calm down.

Your parents had scheduled their trip for next January. My poor Molly, I don't think they're about to go.

Your surgeon suggested to those close to you that they install a hotline to your bedside. Now there's a phone number your friends can call. It's connected to an answering machine that invites people to leave a message for you. A device regularly plays them out loud in your room, in the hope that you'll recognize these voices and that they'll help you resurface, return to where you lost consciousness.

A beautiful idea that made me enthusiastic on the spot. To talk to you, finally! After eight weeks of silence, what a relief! In principle, it was a great idea.

In reality it was another story. I hung up several times without leaving a message. I could not afford to sob as I spoke, or let myself be carried away with emotion, rage, grief. But how could I sound cheerful, like somebody doing well in the best of worlds? What could I say to you, aside from some banalities: "It's me, I miss you, thinking of you, if you only knew how impatient I am to come and see you and hold you in my arms . . . OK, uh, well, kisses and see you soon, my darling ostrich, take care of yourself." Pitiful . . .

It's not a question of leaving you any stressful messages. It's just a matter of sending you regards, in hopes that hearing those whose identity is associated with these voices in a dormant corner of your brain will make memory return. Or at least that some of these recollections are prodding you, because who knows what's become of your memory bank, your brain? How to lift that trapdoor, that leaden silence keeping you in this perverse state of sleep? Can our voices pull off a miracle like the one brought about by the kiss of Benoît's Prince Charming? Is there a secret formula that can put an end to your coma, Molly, and break this spell?

FOR LACK OF POSITIVE MESSAGES TO DELIVER TO YOU IN A TONE MORE OR LESS NATURAL, we've had the idea of enlisting some people from your photos, those VIPs who were kind enough to ask for news of you to begin with. We've drawn up a list of your fifteen favorite personalities, the ones whose voices we think you'd be most likely to recognize, and we've supplied them with that magic telephone number that we were having more and more trouble dialing ourselves. The most famous blonde in French film has even left you a long message.

When I think that it's thanks to Tom Cruise that we met... I was working for a movie magazine, and you were a publicist. Tom Cruise was insisting on some absurd requirements in exchange for the sale of a series of photos of him that I urgently needed because we were finalizing the issue. You'd listened uncomplainingly to me defending my point of view. Then, in a very calm voice, in contrast with my stridency, you'd said to me, "So I'm going to explain to him that you accept all his conditions and I'll give you access to the photos. Then, if he sees the magazine, he can blow a gasket about it all by himself because I'm quitting this gig in fifteen days. As a matter of fact, I agree with you: he's unmanageable." A friendship was born.

Since that time, you've changed jobs, and so have I. I counted: we've both been doing the same work for ten years.

Do you remember that young intern last year who sent you a cover letter? You forwarded me a copy of it with the following comments: "He's cute. He thinks we live in the dark and watch masterpieces while we eat popcorn." You'd underlined a sentence in which he explained, "I'm dreaming of spending entire days next to you in the dark."

You ended up letting him come in so you could explain to him that you spent the lion's share of your days hunting down news items in order to find out about films that are being produced, watching stuff that was mostly a chore, and reading screenplays every day that were more often hard to stomach than mind-blowing. That hadn't seemed to discourage him. So you dealt him the death blow by asking him if he liked gambling. Thinking he was giving the right answer, he'd answered that he hated it. That put an end to the interview.

You and I gamble all the time, for real. We take risks, put substantial sums on several projects. We bet on a story, a team whose job it is to tell it. And then the film is shot. We wait with our stomach in knots. When the betting is closed and the film is finished, when it has been released to theaters, the audience returns its verdict. It is only at that point that you know whether you've gambled well, whether you've won or lost. You call that having *the knack*. The trick, the mojo. But you need luck as well. It's the reason why you always wear a charm bracelet on your right wrist. I remember a tiny cube of dice, a miniature fish, a key, an imp. If you come out of this, I'll have a little four-leaf clover made for you. Me, the person who has never found one.

For many years, you've had your room at my place, and your habits. In Manhattan, you found me a hotel around the corner from your office. We're always together at film festivals, except at night, because your messiness and my fussiness don't go hand in hand, and our jet lag is never in sync, so one of us would keep the other from sleeping. Most of the time you're ahead of me because of jet lag and the fact that you travel more often. As was the case in London recently, we spend ten or so days one-on-one, five or six times a year, a united front against the rest of the profession, seeing and discussing films. And now, I'm preparing to go without you to a festival where I'm going to feel lost, where everybody is going to ask me for news of you, and where I can't imagine not having you beside me.

I'm probably going to get to know that young assistant you just hired. ("Hallelujah! He's an ace backgammon player!" you'd said.)

Don't worry, I'm going to help him, enough so that he can stand in for you, but not too much, so that he won't imagine he could take your place.

While waiting to leave for London again, I ended up being taken along on a side trip for people from the film world to Saint Petersburg, a place I'd never been. You often went to the Moscow Film Festival, which takes place every year in July, but you didn't tell me anything about it, except that year when you'd fallen in love with an actor who you said was young enough to be your son, which made you hold back.

I'm very uncomfortable here, despite the beauty of the city, and I think you would have felt the same. The younger jet set sends even more shivers down my spine in this country than it does elsewhere. The women have a heady beauty, but there's nothing relaxed about it. It seems to be a very concrete form of currency. What the men are thinking is written on their faces. Face and neck are squashed into a single severe mass, and there's a restrained violence that their tailored suits don't soften. Molly, don't be shocked, but at the point we've reached, I figure that it's time to have all religions start contributing. I managed to give the group the slip this morning, enough time to go and light a candle for you in a tiny, freezing cold, jam-packed Orthodox church.

The congregation was composed of old women whose religious fervor blew me away. The beauty of the chants, the intensity of the faces; it wasn't that different from Tarkovsky's films. Since you've been in that elsewhere I find inexplicable, I've thought more about Bergman, Fellini, Lynch,

Wenders, Huston, Visconti, and Truffaut than about more contemporary directors. Just as in literature, the classics are a better refuge, because of their crystal-clear lucidity and amused humanity.

A half hour went by, and I couldn't leave that church. I lingered on the steps by the entrance, caught by the beauty of the chants, intoxicated by the incense, bewitched by the sound of a bell hanging from a chain that a priest shook.

I've never gone with you to pray. Even to a synagogue. You've explained to me a hundred times that you're not a believer. That you don't succumb, as I do, to the beauty of the liturgical chants. But you turned on the waterworks when Elton John sang "Candle in the Wind" at Lady Di's funeral.

We were at the Toronto Film Festival that day, or rather that night. Because of the time difference, it was three in the morning when the broadcast began. A giant screen had been set up in the largest stadium in the city to show the ceremony, and you'd insisted on going. The crowd was unbelievable. Young people, old people, children in strollers, kids on their bikes. You'd brought sandwiches and a thermos of coffee. It was like a kind of mourning festival. All the smells you'd associate with celebration: food, beer, people lying down and smoking grass. But the faces looked trans-fixed, frozen with grief. In the stadium, the sob-bing spilled out in sheets, like a giant wave of tears. Your comments jumped from one subject to another, from the dignity of the two boys, so tiny behind their mother's casket, to the beauty of Nicole Kidman on the arm of Tom Cruise; from the noticeable absence of Stanley Kubrick, who'd been filming with them in the greatest secrecy for the last year, to the surprising appearance of Steven Spielberg, who'd made the trip. Only Elton John succeeded in interrupting your chatter. On the way back, you pointed out the windows that were still lit up. "You see, nobody is sleeping, everyone watched. It reminds me of when Neil Armstrong walked on the moon. I was seven, and it was the first time my parents had let me stay up that late." You asked me if I would have let my children stay up all night to watch the funeral, and when the answer, "Of course not!" popped out of my mouth, you howled with laughter and called me a "French tight-ass." You were right: if it hadn't been for you, I would have missed that strange moment, suspended in time, that planetary communion.

Also in Toronto, I can remember an Indian summer a few years later that was especially mild, with a cloudless blue sky. We were having breakfast on a terrace. In the café, a television screen above the bar was playing. It was on mute and tuned to CNN. Suddenly a voice yelled from inside: *Holy shit!* And the sound was turned up full blast. Ten minutes later, you were spelling out that name for me that sounded like *Aladdin* — bin Laden. Your cell phone had lost its signal, as was the case for many devices dependent on a US transmitter, but mine, which used a French number, was still functioning. I was able to reach my office in Paris, and my assistant managed to call your parents at their home and let you speak to them. Thirty minutes later, nothing was working any more. We were cut off from the rest of the world. We felt as if we were in a film in which every image had been slowed down. Reality was distorted. Traffic was moving slowly. Every driver seemed to have succumbed to the same curse: they seemed dazed, their windows open, their radios at top volume. All of them weren't listening to the same station, but for some strange reason the racket was reassuring. It produced an illusion of everyday normality.

Like all the New Yorkers, you hurried to rent a car. You left in the afternoon. I remember walking for a long time on sidewalks that were abnormally empty, passing stores that were closed, terraces that were deserted. Everyone was home, with their family. I spent the evening alone in my hotel room, sprawled in front of the television, thinking of my children. You waited in line all night to cross the border.

THIS MORNING CLARA ASKED ME WHY YOU AND I WERE FRIENDS. I told her I couldn't explain it. But I spent the day asking myself that same question. Why do you, the American, the pragmatist, the business-woman, the softhearted girl, occupy such a place in my life?

In no particular order:

Because you make me laugh, because you move me.

Because you're indefatigable.

Because you always bring me back a souvenir from the countries you go to without me.

Because you know how to give presents that are unbelievable. I'll never be without that ivory ball inside a black lacquered box that gives off a vanilla fragrance. I don't know where you came across it, nor how the idea came to you. You gave it to me "for inspiration," and for the last fifteen years I haven't written a single line without having it next to me.

Because you never forget a special occasion or a birthday.

Because you love soul music, like me, and really soft pillows, peonies, hot water bottles, and earrings.

Because at every film festival we attend together, you find the best Japanese, the best cappuccino, the best bookstore, and because you send updates every year.

Because you know how to fix my telephone and my computer.

Because at the bottom of your bag you always have tissues, batteries, candy, Advil, a nail file, a bookmark, and a packet of Tabasco sauce, because you think there's never enough in a Bloody Mary.

Because you know how to do card tricks.

Because you can put on nail polish in the back of a moving car without spilling it.

Because you have a good sense of direction.

Because you always read my horoscope when you read yours.

Because you never wear eye makeup but do put on lipstick, and I do the opposite.

Because your French is nonexistent, and I love to speak to you in English.

Because I can tell you everything.

WE'VE NEVER SPENT NEW YEAR'S EVE TOGETHER. When that date comes, you're always in the sun, at the other end of the world, getting a tan. It's your favorite pastime. You've always made fun of my enthusiasm for the Atlantic coast. "Me, I love it when the water's seventy-seven degrees, the temperature's ninety-five, and my suntan oil has zero-degree protection." When I call you, as the clock strikes twelve, we usually sing together, butchering the chorus from Otis Redding's "New Year's Resolution": *"Let's make promises that we can keep."*

This year it's five minutes past midnight. For once I'm listening to the original version of the song, a duet with Carla Thomas, and I'm thinking of you.

What promises can I make you? What can I swear without lying to you? Tell you that you're going to wake up and that life will return to normal? I'm less and less sure of that. The people taking care of you think you're taking a lot of time to come back to life. One thing has been established: they've tried everything, nothing more can be done. Your life is in your own hands. Are you even in a state where you can know that?

This evening, your number wasn't working. That has to be a blunder on the part of the nurse, who obviously forgot to set the answering machine. I'm sure her mind isn't on her work. After all, it's a holiday. She was probably thinking of her evening, of the friends she was going to be with, about what she was going to wear. All of a sudden, I was furious about it. Then I ended up admitting to myself that not being able to leave a message was awfully convenient for me.

It's two in the morning. Everybody is asleep. I'm nibbling those chocolate-covered coffee beans that you're wild about. I'd give anything for this new month that just started to be the one when you wake up and come back, the month of your resurrection.

While waiting, I wish you everything you want, everything you would desire if you were here to desire something. All I can promise is what I'm sure of because it depends only on me: I'll be there for you, whatever happens.

If only you'd please wake up.

YOU SAID YOU'D TRIED EVERYTHING TO GET RID OF YOUR MIGRAINES. Changing glasses, mattresses, perfumes. Sleeping with the windows open. Washing your hair in cold water. Staying away from peanuts, white wine. Fleeing underfloor heating. You tried alternative therapies: acupuncture, relaxation therapy, osteopathy. Massaged your temples with essential oils. Plunged your head into an ice bucket . . . How many hours have you lost lying in the dark with a mask over your eyes, waiting for the attacks to end?

You tried all the formulas, followed all the advice, except for mine: get an MRI.

The idea of the test freaked you out. You said you didn't trust the concept of magnetic waves. That it had to be dangerous to your health. You claimed you were too claustrophobic to go and lie down inside that long white tube, even though you'd never had the experience beyond watching it on a movie screen.

You finally made an appointment.

You never went to it.

The day before you were hospitalized, you saw your company's doctor. He suggested a nasal spray for sinusitis. He told you to slow down on the cappuccinos because your blood pressure was too high.

He didn't prescribe putting your head in a machine to find out what was happening there, or try to understand why you had been suffering almost every day for the last ten years.

He should have.

During all those years, the blood was pounding against your temples. It was flowing in slow motion, drop after drop. A bit like the sand in your plastic bottle that ended up cracking.

An MRI would have detected the danger lying in wait for you, shown that it was necessary to operate immediately, to hold back the blood.

There was a bomb in your head, my darling ostrich.

A membrane was torn. The blood spread into your brain.

It's called an aneurysm.

Last night I dreamed of you. You looked very elegant in one of those austere pantsuits that you're fond of, with a perfect cut. It was a silvery chestnut color, and underneath it the collar of a cream-colored silk blouse could be seen. You'd braided your long hair. Your shoes were high lace-ups in chocolate patent leather. A pair brought back from Italy, where you'd just been. While you were telling me about your trip to Rome where you'd seen a first rough cut of a film, we were walking down a hallway; you pushed open a door and we sat down at a conference table where we were joined by other people. I was sitting next to you, and we were listening to someone speak, when suddenly you stood up, violently pushing back your chair, and shouted, "Look!" You were talking about your hands, which you were holding out in front of you. Everyone noticed how much they were trembling. Then you fainted. I screamed and the sound woke me up.

Maybe that's what should be done: shouting at you, instead of just staying muffled in silence, which is what I imagine your family is doing as they sit beside your bed. They often say you should frighten people with the hiccups, so the shock cuts off their breath and suppresses the spasm that is contracting their diaphragm. If I were alone with you, I'd grab you hard, shake your arm, and scream at you with all my strength, "Wake up!"

I'VE LEFT PARIS FOR SUNDANCE. Usually I arrive in New York in mid-January in the afternoon and we spend the evening together before flying to Utah, where we rent a car to get to this festival and spend ten days together there.

This time I could have taken a direct flight like the other French buyers. But since I can't see you, I want to meet those close to you.

I have dinner with Suzie. Out of your New York friends, she's the one you've talked about most often. She's blond, of Yugoslavian extraction. Her handshake is more efficient than warm, and her face looks tense, as if she's watching out for something. This isn't the kind of girl with whom you can imagine gabbing until dawn. But the stiffness of her bearing forces me to get a grip and to choke back the sobs that rise in my throat when she speaks about you.

She tells me about what is going on behind the scenes at your hospital, the administrative hurdles your parents have encountered. She talks mostly about them, whom I don't know and don't dare call. Your father is the more shaken of the two. That surprises me. I would have thought that since he's a dentist he'd be familiar with the medical world and better equipped to deal with it. What's happening is the opposite. Apparently, your mother is as worried about him as about you. He feels guilty about not having made you take the tests that, like me (I find out), he was urging you to take. It all had to do with his promise to himself to stop meddling with your health.

When you were growing up, he'd had you follow a treatment regime that he claimed strengthened the enamel of your teeth to protect them more effectively against future cavities. It was a brand-new advance in medicine, and he was proud of being able to give you the benefits of it. Ten years later, he'd had to face facts: whereas he couldn't say for certain that the treatment had helped, it was, on the other hand, overwhelmingly clear that swallowing those tablets every week had permanently turned your teeth yellow. Your father had never forgiven himself. Now he was feeling doubly guilty, for having done too much when you were little and not enough since.

I hadn't been aware of the story and found it deeply distressing. If you only knew how difficult it is to be a parent! So many times I've said to my children, "I'm sorry about not being a better mother. It's too bad, but that's the way it is: you ended up with me." It's not an example of me sidestepping the self-satisfaction I really feel, a strategy to make them launch into some overdone denials of what I've just said. I'm saying it because I think it. It's an observation I've ended up becoming resigned to. I'm not the mother I would have wanted to be; nor, even worse, the one I thought I could be. Day-to-day life has eaten away my ambitions, pulled me down a peg or two. Wear and tear, impatience, fatigue, exasperation have gradually whittled away at my reserves of sweetness and understanding, which I'd thought were inexhaustible. The love I have for my children, which sprang up in me at the very second when I knew that they were growing in my belly, is immense, infinite, and inextinguishable. Unfortunately, the qualities that should have flowed from it — patience, calm, control of myself and my nerves — didn't come in addition to it. Instead of them, I'm in possession of reserves of guilt, that frustrating, useless emotion, which renders you lucid and therefore unhappy, but doesn't allow making up for mistakes you've committed nor avoiding committing new ones in the future.

Don't blame your father. Raising someone is permanently fooling yourself. You pass on a sense of ethics, a morality, you create memories. But always with a feeling that it's incomplete, an approximation, a waste. You want so much to do well that you do badly in comparison, too much so. Obviously there's love. But your way of showing it is often awkward, and sometimes destructive. Your father's suffering must be inexpressible.

I take a taxi from the Salt Lake City airport. It's cold and dry. Last year the snow was falling so heavily that you couldn't read the traffic signs. The flight had been late, night had fallen, and I didn't feel at ease at all. You, looking imperial at the wheel of your Lincoln, were whistling, your cigarette and the wheel in your left hand while the right was looking for the radio station with road information, and on the way to that, shutting off the overhead interior light I'd turned on to try to read a road map unfolded on my knees. "You're going to get nauseous! I've already spent the entire flight trying to keep your nose from pouring blood, and my nurse's bag is empty!" I really had spent an hour with an ice cube pressed against my right nostril, which had begun to bleed as soon as we took off.

"Wait, that gives me an idea!" You'd taken out your cell phone to call highway emergency. When they'd arrived ten minutes later, you'd showed them the bloodstained handkerchief as proof of my illness and how urgent it was that I see a doctor in the city. So they'd given us a police escort, and you'd followed them. We'd been the first to arrive at our hotel and were able to get the best rooms. An hour later our suitcases had been put away and we were sitting in front of a gigantic fireplace, sipping our Bloody Marys, while our colleagues and competitors were still struggling along snowy roads.

This evening I have a drink with your work colleagues. Peter, who was once fat — you can tell by his withered cheeks — smokes like a chimney and speaks through his nose. Paul has a body like a rugby player and looks you right in the eye. It's going on twelve years that you've been collaborating with them. We get a kick out of stringing your names together: Peter, Paul, and Molly. Almost like the folk trio who were so popular in the sixties — Peter, Paul, and Mary. I still have the photomontage made of you and your two partners in which you're holding a guitar — you, who have never played any instrument.

I always thought that Peter and Paul were exploiting you. I've often noticed the way they treat you like an underling even though you're partners. They were really lucky to have come across you. You're unmarried, passionate about your work, determined, courageous, and a perfectionist. They're fathers who go home at six to their families, but they've never had any scruples about calling you at inappropriate hours; and you've never dared turn off your cell phone, even on the weekend, in case "the boys" need to reach you.

They tell me that your accident took place right at the moment of the renewal of your agreement with the "major company" with which all of you are affiliated. I knew about that renewal date, which I had thought was further away, and I figured the deadline had been postponed because of circumstances. Not at all. The "boys" negotiated for you, in your place. And they hadn't backed down on anything, refusing to have you excluded from the agreement, even temporarily, or agreeing that your health could be envisioned as a condition for suspension. Quite the opposite. They succeeded in having your name associated with all their decisions, no matter how long you might be absent.

They also arranged for your care to be entirely the firm's responsibility, since your "accident" had happened in your workplace, twenty-four hours after the company doctor had judged your health didn't warrant your stopping working because of illness nor your having any further tests. The fact that this professional had acted so thoughtlessly facilitated the negotiations. Your partners were able to guarantee that your parents wouldn't sue if the firm behaved magnanimously and took care of all the bills that resulted from your condition.

So it was a case of the sordid versus the vile. But at least you're financially protected from now on.

You'd just walked a visitor to the elevators. When you got back to your office, you asked Tom, your new assistant, if he would be nice enough to get you a good cappuccino at the Italian place nearby.

It was raining, and it took him some time to get there and be served. Around twenty minutes. When he got back, he was surprised not to see you. When he came forward to put the cup on your desk, he found you at the foot of your chair, lying on your side along the length of the plate glass window. Unconscious.

It was about six o'clock, the first Thursday in November. An hour must have gone by before a doctor attended to your case. They'd taken you to Lenox Hill Hospital, and your two associates had to be the ones who signed the authorization to open your skull. The surgeon had refused to have your parents called instead: "There's no time. It's probably too late already. If I'm operating, it's because she's forty. If she was ten years older, I wouldn't even try."

The procedure took six hours. The "boys" waited until the next day to call your parents. Forty-eight hours to tell your close friends.

YOU CHOSE WELL WITH TOM. He's exactly as I imagined: slim, elegant, polite. He blushes like a teenager when you look him in the eye. He has a sort of veneration for you. Is it completely sincere or politely hypocritical? He said that he's occupying your chair temporarily but that he's a long way from having the competence required, and that only a combination of circumstances justifies his current position. He's aware of my status as your colleague and friend, but is clever enough not to try to intrude on my memories and make me talk about you. He's warm and professional, ill at ease and touching. I'm certain you have a weakness for him. He's tall, with a handsome smile, a retro side to his style, *Butch Cassidy*, but Newman more than Redford. Completely your type.

Molly, I hate watching movies without you. I miss you. I miss your presence. I miss the smell of chewing gum you chomp on furiously wherever you can't smoke. Depending on the day, it scents your breath with mint, strawberry, or cinnamon. Like your magic pen, which becomes a flashlight when you unscrew it and, when you're bored, allows you to check how long the film we're watching is and at what hour the next one we want to see will start. I love your way of concentrating incredibly hard when you like the film, becoming so motionless that you forget to breathe, and when you finally inhale you do it so deeply that it sounds like snoring.

I miss your professional opinions. The way you look at films has always differed from mine. You're more sentimental, quicker to be moved. Melodramatic pathos, which makes me bristle and immediately alienates me from the story being told, doesn't bother you. Just the opposite — you go for it. Which doesn't prevent you, as soon as the film is over, from appraising it negatively if it's not a film you're planning to buy. That capacity of yours to separate yourself from your own emotions, abandon your identity as a spectator, and put on a buyer's hat, has often irritated me.

How can you *not* take into consideration your own opinion to such a degree?

It's something we've ended up discussing a number of times. That's what I miss the most. Arguing with you. Getting annoyed with you. Finding arguments to oppose yours. Comparing your culture with mine, your sensibility, my sentimentalism and vice versa. Realizing that tastes are formed as a result of our memories, childhoods, wounds, delights; and understanding that there's nothing objective about liking a film. A film speaks to us or it doesn't. It moves us or gets on our nerves. It softens our heart or makes our hair stand on end. That's our job. Choosing one story from all the ones they tell us.

You said that if you ever decide to start your own company, you'll call it Once Upon a Time. You're right: it's a magic saying, the open sesame that makes me get up in the morning.

But tell me, Molly, how can you want me to be interested in the slightest story alone in my chair, while you're lying in a hospital bed in that ultraconventional decor you see in all those

American series where the doctors always end up curing their patients? They're handsome, overworked, omnipotent, fragile. They have our lives in their hands. What about the one who's been looking after you all these months? Which episode is he in? Does he know the story? Is he truly dedicated to it? Does he find you fascinating or hopeless? Does he know — he, at least — if it has a happy ending?

THIS MORNING I WAS TIDYING UP THE CHILDREN'S ROOM, and the big ceramic Pinocchio that watches over Benoît's bed made me think of you. Pinocchio also ended up by accident in the belly of a whale. It closed its mouth around him, and he was imprisoned in its guts. He must have been cold, hungry, and afraid to be plunged into the dark like that. I forget how he got out of there. And what about you? Which belly, inside which giant fish have you gotten lost? However, you're an experienced swimmer. You love underwater diving, and the sea is your element, unlike me whose drowning phobia prevents me from going anywhere that my feet can't touch the ground. Why can't you remember your reflexes? Why don't you make that lifesaving kick that will bring you back to the surface?

But then, you're not a wooden puppet who has to pay for her lies. Isn't this bad joke going to be over soon? What is this bottomless pit of sorrow, sadness, unanswered questions? Hundreds and thousands of questions to avoid asking myself the only one that counts, the same one that in the morning has awoken me with a start for the last three months, after keeping me from sleeping the night before; the same one that, after an hour turning and twisting in my bed on one side and then the other, then on my back, stomach, and then without a pillow, sends me into the bathroom to take a quarter of a tablet in order to dodge that nagging, ridiculous, selfish, inevitable question: Why you and not me? By virtue of what order, what secret arrangement, what great book? What nonsense. Life goes on, life stops. The light turns red or green. The heart beats, then stops beating. At night mine beats too hard. Over where you are, yours is tracing jagged, irregular lines on a machine.

The nights when I don't resort to pills, I look out the window. The neighbors' lights. The shutters, which are open or closed. The lives you can make out. In the building opposite this one, who is going to get sick? Who'll get better? How to stop thinking about it? How to keep from going crazy?

Molly, you love playing cards, and you've drawn the Old Maid. Life's accident. The one each of us fears having. The one that makes voices lower during conversations. Couldn't talking about it bring down bad luck on our heads? So we fall silent, ashamed of admitting that we're relieved to have been spared by someone else's bad luck.

Even your singlehood is playing against your side. To how many of us are you really essential? Aside from your father, your mother, your sisters? No child, fiancé, none of those relationships that people around me are saying it's a relief you don't have in your life. But what if the opposite were true? What if those were the only forms of love that would allow you to find the strength to fight deep inside? And what if friendship, no matter how sincere, isn't enough? What song of what siren could give you the determination, the unremitting will to open the throat of the whale? In the seven notes of the scale, is there a magic combination, a series of sounds to discover, like those François Truffaut invented in *Close Encounters of the Third Kind* to establish a connection with the extraterrestrials? What melody could create a path all the way to your planet Comma?

Not your favorite songs, at any rate; your playlist was already tried, in vain. Soul, blues, light music, the classics, even the original music from your bedside movies. The tape that plays our recorded messages is still sliding off your ears. Like the words of love murmured by your family. On the walls of your room, where I saw photos, there are now film posters, postcards showing your favorite beaches, pictures of your friends, Post-its in every language and color. It's no longer a hospital room but a mortuary room, minus the flowers. We wouldn't have put your funeral service together any differently: favorite songs and poems, the voices of those closest to you. And what if, instead of bringing you back to life, we've been building your tomb?

IT HAPPENED LAST NIGHT. You were alone with your machines. In any case, no human being would have been able to put a finger on that incredible moment that was invisible to the naked eye and that the doctors, like good seismologists, spotted immediately, interpreted, and transmitted to your family.

You have come out of your deep coma and passed into another stage, which indicates that in all likelihood you're going to move through all of them, resurface by plateaus, until you reach the surface of the world, of consciousness, and finally come back to yourself, to us all.

You're finally returning to the world of the living. The doctors say so. But instead of celebrating your return elatedly and holding our breaths impatiently, the way you swell your lungs with all your strength to blow out all the candles on the cake in one breath, our anguished wait has given way to a gnawing anxiety that everyone drags around on his own, which no one can mention, as if verbalizing it was going to make it happen, as if saying the words was going to cast an irremediable jinx on you.

In what kind of state are you returning to us? What traces of this long dive without an Aqua-Lung will you retain? Has planet Comma correctly oxygenated your head and lungs? Have you forgotten anything in the belly of the whale? Is there a price to pay for reassuming human form? Have you had to give up speech, like the little mermaid? Will your body recover all its functions? Is it enough to recharge its batteries, do a reset, as you often did with my cell phone when it wasn't working the way I wanted it to? Are you going to recover completely? Will you, will everything, be "like before"?

MOLLY, I'M WARNING YOU, THE STORY I'M GOING TO TELL
YOU IS APPALLING.

It's banal, clichéd, in bad taste, disgraceful,
shameful, stupid, vulgar, or, as Godard would say,
dégueulasse.

This story has no interest.

But it has become mine.

A nasty business.

All it took was three words on the screen of a
cell phone.

Words loaded with innuendos.

Words speaking of desire, frustration, impatience.

If they'd been on your cell phone, I would have
found it delightful.

These are words that I could have said to the
man I love a long time ago.

The words you say at the beginning, when you can't live without the other person.

Vincent was dozing in the living room. His cell phone, lit up, was lying next to him.

I rushed to it to keep the beep signaling a message from waking him. Didn't have to because he was deep asleep; I'm the one who's always been the light sleeper.

When I read the three words, I let go of the phone, which fell softly onto the couch cushion without breaking.

It was my heart that was in pieces.

"I miss you."

Three words, like the three strikes of a bell in a theater to announce the beginning of a show. Three words that set off an earthquake.

Molly, how can I describe to you what that did to me? Did you have the same symptoms before you lost consciousness? Your body starts to disobey you. It slips away from you. You've lost control of it. Your back curves under the violence of the blow to your solar plexus, and cold makes you go numb. Your jaw hurts from the force of your teeth clenched to keep any sound escaping from your asphyxiated lungs, into which the air has stopped entering. You shake your head to keep the bad thoughts from entering it, but they've already invaded everything.

Molly, honestly, at that exact moment, I would have willingly changed places with you, to keep from feeling that sludge sucking me up and thrusting its way into me, that rage, that disappointment, that anger, that powerlessness. I would have wanted to smash that telephone and lose consciousness. Disappear into that planet Comma where the loss of consciousness that anesthetizes the mind perhaps would have prevented me from suffering.

I, who always claimed that jealousy was foreign to me, am now discovering that it's a rat, a worm, something indefinable but physical gnawing away at the insides of my intestines, burning the digestive tube, sending acid into my throat, paralyzing my limbs and ravaging my brain. Which has suddenly been emptied of all its data — to devote itself compulsively to the study of a single piece of it, to the dissection of one obsessive thought.

I was the confident half of a couple I thought was happy.

I was an imbecile, Molly, I know now.

I didn't want to see, guess, feel anything.

I was curled up comfortably in my placid sense of content.

Coming to is brutal.

The rat has moved into my entrails. I can feel it making itself at home.

Molly, you're the only one I can tell this to — this story.

It makes me feel ashamed.

At least I've avoided that bad made-for-TV-movie suspense where the deceived wife tries to find out who the other woman is. There was a name attached to the three words, a name I know. The enemy has a face. Sometimes I see her at conferences, dinners. One student among many, one of the multiple variations of a model renewed every school term and nearly unchanging through the years: young, impressed, admiring, wanting to be noticed and achieving it, but in vain, since noticed does not mean esteemed. Vincent has never been taken in by the students fluttering around him, not that this prevents him from purring with pleasure when one of the more ravishing, sassier, cleverer of them corners his attention for the span of a dinner. On those evenings, as I've already explained to you, I'd rather slip away and go home alone, try to convince myself that my leaving has perhaps ruined a bit of the simpleminded pleasure Vincent takes in feeling devoured by eyes. I can describe to you what comes next. He'll drink a little too much, come back careful not to make any noise, but never miss banging against the foot of the bed. Then he'll fall asleep immediately, wake up looking pasty, shamefaced and falsely contrite, and try to prove to me with anecdotes how lost but how nice that poor girl was, a little silly, but rather entertaining; and he'll leave it at that, comforted by the certainty that I've already let him off the hook, forgotten the end of an evening so devoid of interest that it only provoked indifference on my part. And it's true that I'd gotten into the habit of thinking of these young girls with amused condescension, that I pitied such creatures for imagining an affair with their French literature teacher was possible, as if whoever it was could meddle with our intimacy, bolstered as it was by twenty years of cozy complicity.

Molly, you've always lived alone, and you were living well. You would say that it was too late, that you couldn't adapt any longer to someone else's ways. However, with time, living as a couple becomes comfortable — believe me. The other person has adapted to your habits and accepted your eccentricities. After a certain number of years, worry, irritation, any form of emotion likely to start a discussion that could grow into a conflict loses urgency and intensity.

You substitute a sluggish acceptance of the other person's thinking for your need to speak your mind no matter what or show how you're different. When you know the other person to the point of guessing what will make him fly off the handle, you've reached a time when it's less of a kick but more advisable not to argue. What good is displaying your point of view when you can guess which arguments are going to be used to counter it, when you know that when you're finished each of you will feel that much more offended because the issue can't be settled?

Decorating your apartment took up all your time and energy in the weeks before your coma; well, two people living together evolves the way a living room gets furnished. You move from confrontation, with each of you sitting opposite the other in a chair, your spines very straight and wedged against the chair back, to more of a slump that feels ever so much more comfortable, on a two-person sofa on which each has his favorite side, just like the bed you share to such an extent that instead of looking at each other, you're both looking at the same wall. Renouncement means the absence of argument and leads to forgetting to discuss anything at all. You stop asking the other person his opinion; you simply want to keep track of his state of mind: "You all right?" "Yes, what about you? Everything OK?"

Each has blunted his claws. However, life hasn't lost its harshness. Battles grow more numerous outside, with others. So, when you're home, you long for a little peace and quiet to replenish your strength. You savor the harmony, the feeling of well-being. With both of you having reached the summit, it's sweet to take a breath together, side by side, before climbing back down the mountain. You take the time to live, before watching yourself grow old.

You and I had that conversation again very recently, in London. I was explaining to you that Vincent and I were coming out of that trouble spot you encounter when the children are very little, that time was flying by fast and moving pretty much in a straight line, that Benoît and Clara were getting bigger and taking up all the room there was, and that they were also practically the only cause of our arguments.

A student. Can you imagine how ridiculous that is? What does he talk to her about? What does a barely legal teenager understand about the problems of an adult's life? How could she change the course of an existence like Vincent's, which is so full already?

I'm asking you that question. It helps me. It reminds me of what I'm sure of, something three words on a cell phone have chucked out the window.

I know what your answer is.

Opposites attract. That's what it's about.

Obviously. It's stupid to cry. She's young, free, available. Getting involved with her is coming closer to a world where everything is possible because it all still remains to be lived. For Vincent, it's as if he'd discovered that he had the use of a pause button. It's our family life that he's bringing to a standstill. He's gone off the beaten path. He's experimenting. He's discovering the pleasure of wasting time, frittering it away, squandering it. And in this unhoped-for time he's discovering and taking a kind of pleasure whose taste, fragrance, memory he'd lost track of. It's from a fleeting period when nothing weighed on you, hurried you, where every day was like an open window and your own desire was law, where you went forward and faced the rest of the world with a swagger. It's a time that neither you nor I really savored, because we were in such a hurry to learn, understand, accumulate experience; and now Vincent is rediscovering it with delight, now that he's an adult. He needs to fill his lungs with that ultrahackneyed elixir so distrusted by those who've left it forgotten behind them. And I've suddenly discovered, Molly, that I'm one of them. It's so very simple. This isn't a demon, it's a rediscovery. For Vincent, it's unexpected. Youth. Feeling young again. Giving yourself the illusion that life is a road still to embark upon, when in reality, you've already covered half the path. How could it be possible to resist such a temptation?

There were other students before. Some even more beautiful, more brilliant, more available. But it wasn't the right moment.

Why now? Now, exactly? Our life is pleasant, our children thriving . . . our family harmonious . . . Is the fact that everything is so calm what's boring him? I never imagined that this stability we built together could fulfill me to such a degree and weigh on him so terribly. I don't know when we stopped having the same dreams. You see, while I was only seeing us, he began to question himself. While black screens were telling me stories, he was rethinking his.

Molly, tell me the truth, have I become that conventional mother who's blind and deaf? Have I become that cliché? Such a bad farce? Really? Since when?

You know how much I hate reading that kind of predictable scenario. The husband, the wife, and the other woman, that intruder who embodies the serpent of temptation.

In that type of story, the resolution is completely binary. Like your two-column sheet. For or against?

Say something or keep quiet.

Leave or stay.

Protest or forgive.

Suffer or forget.

Molly, what would you say in my place? Enough is enough or more?

As you're finally coming back from your planet Comma, I'm going out on the attack, in a land that was unknown to me and that I thought I'd never have to visit someday. I have no choice. I have to confront it. Jealousy. That bad counselor. That scorching lava that blinds the senses and muddles the brain. If I surrender to it, I'm done for.

FOR THE MOMENT, I'M KEEPING MY MOUTH SHUT. I'm much too crazed to start the battle. I'm not armed for that kind of combat. Quite the opposite — it feels like all my strength has left me. During the day, I deal with it. I have no choice in front of the children. At night, I drift from one nightmare to another. I dream we're divorcing, that I'm single again, that I'm invited to dinners where they seat me at the end of the table, that I go out with men I don't know anything about, and to whom I have nothing to say. I understand that you're supposed to talk, to explain who you are, to seduce, to sell yourself, but I'm not capable of it. I live alone. Vincent has made a new life for himself, but I can't stop undoing mine. You're going to laugh; in my dreams I've changed occupations. I've become a librarian, and I've got all the answers when it comes to the books in the romance section. Some nights, I've gained forty-five pounds. On others, I'm anorexic, have lost my teeth, my hair. I smoke filterless Gitanes and live in bed. In the morning, I wake up crying, but I feel Vincent's breath on the nape of my neck, so I hurry out of bed to keep him from noticing how red my eyes are.

I haven't said anything, haven't made the slightest remark; but it's obvious to me that I'm different. I've stiffened. Vincent must have guessed that I'm not myself. He seems particularly considerate. In normal times, I would have said thoughtful, but now I see him more as attentive, as if he were on his guard and had a foreboding of everything I've guessed.

Everything is so crystal clear when I think about it! I'm an idiot, Molly. I would have made a lousy detective. How couldn't I have noticed that Vincent, who never knew where he'd put his cell phone, now never lets it out of his sight? It's with him everywhere, even — and especially — in the bathroom, where the flowing of the faucets is getting noisier and noisier. No, I'm not paranoid. It's simply that all these things I hadn't noticed, at least not consciously, are exploding in my brain and in front of my eyes in very big close-ups, in

3-D and Technicolor. Vincent forgets his doctors' appointments, a hypochondriac like him; but it does occur to him to stop in for a haircut, whereas usually I have to force him to do that. He's wearing a new cologne, despite the fact that he used to swear only by his Penhaligon's English Fern, which the two of us went and bought for him in London, and that you insisted on paying for because you'd forgotten his birthday. He has bought a collection of shirts, even though he hates wearing new clothes. He's jaunty, absentminded, flippant. More than anything, I sense he's unavailable, faraway, vague, elsewhere . . .

I'm losing faith, can no longer hope that tomorrow will be another day. I'm out of patience. You know my motto: The best defense is to attack. It isn't very far away from yours: The best way out is always through.

Molly, I've got to act, make a decision, do something. I can't stand waiting any longer. Waiting for you to wake up. And waiting for him to announce his desires to me.

Since I sense that he wants to be able to do as he pleases, I leave him alone. Never mind if it's suicidal. I'm the one who leaves. I'm traveling more and more, to the great displeasure of the children, who hate to see me go and start sulking as soon as they catch sight of my little red suitcase, the one I take out when I'm traveling without them. Benoît opens the drawers, helps me with a sad look, whereas Clara, who is always more drastic, runs away to entangle herself in our nanny Lala's apron strings, who will toss her some crepes whenever as she thinks Clara is sad. And it enrages me to see her stuffing my daughter like that, but I can read in her eyes that if I wasn't absent so often, she wouldn't need to give her substitute pleasures. So I let her go ahead with it, feeling contrite, guilty.

My life feels like water flowing from my clenched fist as I try in vain to hold on to it. I'm running away. Without you, Molly, I don't know where to turn. You're the only person I can tell all this to.

I think I've never felt so alone.

I sleep in impersonal hotel rooms in which I burn incense that Vincent is crazy about and that makes me feel like I'm home. I try to escape through the films I'm watching, but now I can't stand any of them. The comedies exacerbate me, the misunderstandings are oppressive, the cross-purposes give me a stomachache, the dramas bore me, the science fictions fill me with anguish. I'm not interested in any kind of thriller. I'm focused on the burdens in my own life, my marriage, my family. The future terrifies me, Molly. A life without him? It doesn't make sense.

You're finally conscious, finally awake, finally allowed to see a few visitors.

I'm coming!

I'm so delighted to be going to your bedside before everybody. Only your family and the boys have this privilege. I've promised to give your three other friends news about you, to call them as soon as I leave the hospital.

This morning I got up very early, printed out these pages; and I put them in an envelope the same bright pink color as your baggage labels. I'm sure it's going to make you burst out laughing. I've just deleted the parts about Vincent. For the time being, to hell with my married life. You're the one who counts, you, my enduring spirit. You stayed lost for more than three months on your planet Comma; you've practically beat all records, but we're going to forget fast about all of that.

Molly, I'm too excited to have the patience to reread what I've written. All of these sentences are probably meaningless now that you've woken up. I'll bring them to you anyway. It's my way of showing you in concrete terms that I didn't stop thinking of you.

I don't know a thing about what state you're in. I don't want to think about it. I want to see you and decide for myself how you seem to me. I know that you became conscious again three weeks ago, that you recognized your family. You were transferred to another hospital two hours away from Manhattan. I don't know if you were told of my visit. I hope not. You've always adored surprises.

My head's spinning, my ears ringing, my throat dry. Visits aren't allowed after six p.m. I didn't even take the time to stop by the hotel and drop my suitcase off. In any case, the instructions are not to stay in your room more than fifteen minutes, because you're too tired to sustain a conversation. My hands are sweating. I'm shaking a little. If the taxi driver were a smoker, I think just this once I would have asked him for a cigarette.

Have you gone back to smoking? Have they cut your hair? And your fingernails? They must be long; for once you weren't able to bite them. Have you lost weight, gained it? Do you already have permission to wear one of your pairs of striped men's pajamas that I love, or are you wearing an off-white hospital gown like the ones in those American films, the kind that are tied with a knot at the left side? I realize that I've avoided imagining you concretely until now. My legs are giving way. You're the one who's sick, and I'm the one who's afraid.

The taxi driver tells me that he's very familiar with the route to the medical center, that it's a renowned establishment that specializes in extensive rehabilitation. What's he talking about? What does it mean? That ready-made expression annoys me. What's the meaning of such an impenetrable adjective? *Extensive*. Is it a PC word to avoid saying *serious*?

I half-open the window and breathe the humid air. It won't be long before it snows. I close my eyes. I've never so much wanted to have faith as I do at this second.

For pity's sake, make it be that you're well.

It was the girl at reception who called the taxi to take me back. The driver must be used to it. He made note of the address, turned his music all the way up, and belted into the night without so much as a look at me. Curled up in back, I watch the scenery flash by. I would really like to cry, which would soothe me. I can't. I spend the trip bushed, frozen stiff, moving my head slightly to the rhythm of the potholed road and the monotonous Hindu tunes the driver hums along with.

It doesn't bother me. It keeps me from hearing the sounds of the car.

Your voice is playing in a loop in my ears.

A thick voice that croaks to me, "You know I almost died?"

You repeated that to me four times.

You're just at the start of discovering the fear that made us tremble for so many months.

For you, this is an enormous, astounding piece of information.

You almost died, and you can't get over it.

When I entered your room, as soon as you saw my face, you let out a kind of minicry, held out your hand, your cheek, breathed in my perfume and recognized it, which made you smile. You smiled with your eyes, and I nearly burst into tears. I don't think it surprised you to see me, and I sensed that it was giving you pleasure. You murmured my name, but your reedy voice was so thin, so close to inaudible, that I came very close to you and bent to speak to you in your ear. You were listening to my words, blinking, nodding, your eyes shining.

I didn't take out the pink envelope from my bag to put it on the bedside table, which was already too crowded. It would have seemed incongruous in this spartan room with its flaking paint, medical smell, lack of ventilation, and underfloor heating, which was already drying out my mucous membranes.

I did my best not to let you see the shock that I felt in discovering you on this metal bed.

My Molly, they've massacred your hair, cut it at every angle, which isn't serious; but your face . . . has gotten so drawn. It's still pallid, almost translucent. It's a face snatched from death but not yet returned to life, a face with ringed eyes in which I can read a terrible fear that goes right into me and punches a hole in my stomach. You try to make the half gesture of a kiss, but your lips have trouble grazing my cheek.

Your mother, who is at your bedside as I'd expected, gets up to meet me. She's shorter than you, heavier, too, especially in that beige suit that's too tight for her. She's just as you have always described her, with auburn hair that has too much hairspray, hoop earrings, a "French manicure," and misshapen athletic shoes. She takes me in her arms as if I were a family member, interrupts me as soon as I greet her: "Oh no, no 'Mrs.' between us. You *must* call me Dora," and then takes control of the conversation. She's staying at a hotel very nearby, not even five minutes by car, and luckily, right across the street, there is a "wonderful steakhouse" where she's a regular customer. Your father can only spend time with you on weekends, whereas she's at your side "around the clock." This gives her a chance to have continuous contact with the medical team that is treating you. "And thanks to them, Molly is going to make *so much* progress!" Her forced enthusiasm is oppressive. It's as if her mouth were sucking in all the air in the room.

You have closed your eyes. I come and sit down next to you. I take your right hand. I can feel it trembling in mine. Your left hand is resting on the sheet. It isn't moving. Your mother covers it with hers. "And all this is going to take *a little* time." She looks me straight in the eye. I get the impression she's trying to tell me something. I don't see what it could be.

The nurse enters without knocking, and from her stony face I understand I should leave. I get up quickly, bend over you, and murmur a few more words into your ear. I tell you how much I care about you, Molly, my Molly, I love you so much. I can feel your breath against my cheek. As I've always done because that habit amuses you, I add, "And quick, my two Parisian kisses."

I place my lips against your cheeks.

One of them is very warm, the other not at all.

Your mother is still staring at me. Her eyes move from me to your left hand, still lying on the sheet. It hasn't moved since I came into your room.

Your unmoving hand. Your cold cheek.

Your inert leg under the blanket.

Your mouth, Molly, a corner of which does not manage to smile.

Peter and Paul say they had decided not to warn me so that I'd be as natural as possible in front of you. They were even hoping that the visit would be too brief for me to have the time to notice what was going on. In any case — and Peter's voice over the telephone increases in volume, as if that would make it easier to convince me — the doctors haven't lost hope about seeing you regain the feeling on your left side. That's the reason you've been transferred to this special unit. With intense rehabilitation, they say that they can obtain unexpected results. A real battle awaits you, and you will all wage it together.

Seated in front of my computer, I type these words the way tears spill out, without stopping, almost without breathing.

I no longer know very well exactly whom I write to.

To you, of course.

But not to the person I saw today, who wasn't moving, as if she'd been washed up onto her overly stiff bed. To that person, I can't. Let's just say that for the time being, I'm speaking to your brain, which is functioning very well. You recognized me, asked me right away for news of Vincent and the children without mistaking their names; and you even remembered that Benoît was going to be six. I saw — or at least sensed — the glimmer of the old Molly in your eyes. Even if your voice has changed, even if those eyes appear haunted by a terror that seemed inexplicable to me until I noticed your left hand, I know that deep inside you're still there.

I've found you again, incredibly fragile and battered, but still near and still so familiar. I've missed you so much.

Describing my visit to anyone at all is out of the question. I'd rather turn off my laptop. Taking a small break is also prolonging the illusion for a few more hours of the Molly your three friends are hoping to see again. What can I tell them without lying? The truth?

I would have liked to record the following message for those who'll call the hospital for news of you: "Molly is not here for the moment.

She's away from herself. If you're looking for her, it would be better to find her again in your memories."

Mine have disappeared, momentarily erased by your distorted voice that murmured in my ear, "You know I almost died?"

Tonight, I'm not there for anyone.

Four in the morning. Impossible to sleep. Lying in front of a nonstop news channel, I cut off the sound and play devil's advocate. I put myself in your place. When you're an adult, independent, a globe-trotter, and you find yourself infantilized by an overprotective mother and a glum nurse; when you're in shock about what has happened, and you find yourself dependent upon a body that you can't control as you did before; when your brain is laboring to process all this new data, can you find the energy in yourself to wage such a struggle? Poor Molly, you seem so destitute. Even the modulation of your voice has changed. It seemed more muffled, lower.

Normally, I would have called Vincent to tell him everything. But I can't handle speaking to him.

I don't know how to behave with him any more. There are few possible options and — you know me — I've already imagined all the scenarios. Confronting him will be a relief for me but will free him from the fear that he might have of hurting me. With no more need to conceal things, maybe he will want to live this story even more fully? Keeping quiet would require a superhuman effort on my part. I'm afraid resentment is making me aggressive, which is bringing grist to the other woman's mill, as she already has the advantage of being the younger one and now would also become the nicer one.

Molly, you've often criticized me for this, and you certainly are right, but I'm so used to reasoning in reference to him, from a point of view in which he's included, by taking him into consideration! He's my partner, my foundation, my base, the direction in which I aim all my serves. For the first time in twenty years of life together, I find myself alone on the court without him standing on the other side of the net. And I'm not talking to you about the children. Can a couple make themselves suffer without them becoming the collateral victims? If that were possible, it would be known.

Already they're complaining that I'm away too often ...

Molly, I never told you about that famous night. I'm not boasting about it. I'm much too ashamed. The worst night of my life as a mother. The one when I felt stupendously guilty. Clara was barely three years old. She was in bed with a fever. I heard her coughing in her sleep. I opened the door of her room and bent over her bed. She opened her eyes; but instead of snuggling up in the arms I held out for her, she turned on her side, her expression shut me out, and she whined, "Not you. I want Lala." I stood firm. I explained that at night the Lalas of the entire world were sleeping, whereas the moms got up no matter what time it was to give cuddles and take care of boo-boos. She ended up letting herself be cuddled and fell asleep again against my chest. I listened to her breathing, curled up against me. I felt her fevered head against my neck, and I took stock of the extent of the damages. Being able to juggle a profession and a family life was a myth; then, an illusion. A child doesn't relate to the concept of a proxy. She needs you, body and soul. If you're not there, she'll need someone else. That's the way it is. Nature abhors a vacuum.

All the same, books dedicated to child raising hammer one thing in: it's important for children to have a mother who is fulfilled. And what if the thing that fulfills me isn't taking care of my children exclusively from morning to night, but also working, traveling, using my brain cells, and experiencing life on my own? That's too bad, but that's what Lalas were invented for. They're hard to find; they make themselves indispensable, hold you hostage, and take your place in the hearts of your children. They possess the key to the harmony of your family, a key worth its weight in gold; and you willingly pay the price for it, without understanding that you're losing more than they are getting from it. Of course, there is life outside of them: Sundays, holidays, vacations, and school. Little by little, time will pass and children will grow. One day, Lalas will leave your home. Then it will be your children who will leave.

In the meantime, a pattern has been established. Your absences. Your negligence.

There it is, Molly. Something you've escaped. It's the lot of mothers who work. A special tax, a dash of daily anguish added to all the others. Forming a decoction men don't have to stomach.

That night, I was truly aware that you would exchange your life for mine without hesitation; your trauma for my anguish, your concrete fear of tomorrow for my conjugal trivia. With or without Vincent, my future is in front of me. Yours is a nebula that you're in no condition to apprehend.

On the television screen, an ad for Nike is ending on its famous slogan: Just do it. It never struck me how stupid, naive, and untruthful such an expression is. Infuriating. I stretch out my arm to shut those idiots up. When you want to, you can? If only that could be the case for you. You've managed to come back from your planet Comma, Molly. You achieved it all on your own. You'll definitely find a way to overcome this last ordeal in your obstacle course. Won't you?

THREE WEEKS AFTER MY VISIT, YOU STILL DON'T HAVE THE STRENGTH TO ANSWER THE TELEPHONE. I call your mother, Suzie, Tom, and your three European friends, who all ended up making the trip.

Everyone's account is along the same lines.

It's not encouraging.

You spend your time lying down without sleeping, your eyes staring into space. You don't want the television turned on. You don't read the magazines that are brought to you. You don't want anything. Especially not talking. You were able to summon enough energy in yourself to send away the rabbi and the psychologist your mother had called in. You made it understood that she hadn't a clue, that you had nothing to say, to anyone.

You do say that you need to put your thoughts in order.

All you've asked for is your iPod. You listen to music nonstop, the earphones glued to your ears. You're loath for anyone to remove them, even for medical treatments.

You're experiencing head-on the repercussions of your weeks in a coma. You're sizing up the enormity of what has happened to you. Of what is coming. But instead of this giving you a desire to fight, you're not really making an effort. You put up with your daily rehabilitation exercises. The doctors say that your heart isn't in it. You don't believe in it. You aren't fighting. You find the effort too painful, the result too uncertain.

You say that you're ill and that unremitting effort is pointless.

You say that you're too tired, that you can't do it.

Molly, what are you doing?

Don't you understand?

Time, Molly, time is passing, and the days are piling up.

You're not getting any better.

You say you don't give a damn.

The doctors are discouraged. Peter and Paul are becoming pessimistic. Tom is becoming more important every day and, for lack of having been officially hired to do your job, he's replacing you on a day-to-day basis. He says that he comes to see you every three or four days to keep you informed, but that you interrupt him by saying that it no longer interests you. Molly, I can easily imagine that movies are the least of your concerns, but you're being thrown a line to help you come back to us, understand? You've got to grab hold of it, even if you don't feel like it. It's the same with appetite: it's true — I promise — it comes back as you eat.

Molly, I can't believe that you've lost interest in everything apart from chocolate milkshakes. You've got to find a reason inside yourself to fight. Do it for yourself, for us, for the children you don't yet have, for the beaches of the South Seas you haven't yet discovered, for the memories that are still waiting to be made by you, for the years you have left to live. Do it for the miracle your surgeons have accomplished. Do it so that you won't have come back from your planet Comma in vain. Do it to give your life meaning. Do it so we can go back to seeing films and traveling the globe.

No one from the profession is rallying to your cause any more. Now that you've come out of the coma, your case is less interesting. It's no longer a question of life or death. About you they say you've pulled through, that you're resting. Until when? No one knows. No one in the group of people around you will dare to make a prognosis.

The official communiqué from your "major company" states: "We've advised her to take the time she needs to recover." Enough time for everyone to forget you?

I no longer know what to tell you about. Six weeks have passed since I went to see you.

It feels as if I'm writing to your shadow. I'm writing to the Molly you seem not at all in a hurry to become again.

You don't really believe that I'm going to tell you about the vagaries of my days, my meetings, the films I've seen, the dinners I've gone to, the trips I'm planning to take, or other anecdotes that are even more trivial, like the one about my car breaking down in a tunnel today, when I know the ordeals you're going through.

I think about those ordeals all the time. I know that every morning, after the doctor's visit, they come to get you out of bed so that you can try to move your left leg, arm, and hand. They make you work, first lying down and then standing on a treadmill. I know that you tire very easily, that your head spins, that the ground beneath your feet slips away, that you get nauseous and feel like crying. I imagine the conflicting emotions sweeping through you, the determination to get through this, your discouragement about the immense amount of work such a thing entails, your lack of understanding about what has happened to you, the lethargy into which your condition plunges you, the isolation of your room, the permanent presence of a mother you've never felt close to ... I think of you, I visualize you, I imagine you, I feel you, and I experience a pang of anguish. Forgive me, I can't seem to talk to you about anything else. Compared to what you endure each day, my daily life is so laughable ...

I'm also not going to vent my depressing story, tell you about the efforts I make every day not to ask Vincent any questions, the hate his cell phone inspires in me, my sleepless nights, the money I stupidly blow on lavish outfits that I'll never have a chance to wear, just for the pleasure of feeling desirable when I slip into them. I've never spent so much on beauty products, treatments for the face, creams for the body, like a true geisha. Only Clara notices and .registers all these details, which are new for her. The nail polish I put on. The skirts I'm suddenly more willing to wear than my jeans. The hats that, like you, I've begun collecting. My new glasses. Lipstick. She summed it up her way: "Mommy, you're like Babar, you're getting dolled up." Her favorite book is the one in which the elephant has come to the city and buys green suits and patent leather shoes in the department stores. In her eyes, I'm like that pachyderm. She's right. I feel as clumsy and out of place as he did. I'm fighting against the desire to chuck all of it, but I'm trying to put up a good front.

Molly, you'll be glad to learn that I'm following your advice to the letter. You've always claimed that wearing stiletto heels and a tight skirt was like putting on a battle dress that gave you a boost in facing a difficult situation. "It makes me take little steps, pull in my backside, and stand straight with my head high. It's like armor. On five inches, you're a warrior, believe me."

This morning, when I walked into the kitchen, teetering three inches above the floor (I can't manage any higher), Clara studied me from top to bottom and winked at her father. "Daddy, are you jealous?" I opened the refrigerator door to put all that off track and pretended to be looking for the milk, which was already sitting right there on the table. Vincent shrugged indifferently. Clara insisted: "Well, Daddy?" Vincent stroked her head. "No, my princess. Jealousy doesn't do any good." He looked at me with a scoffing smile and added, "But you're right, Mommy looks very stylish this morning." I kept my eyes on the coffeepot. Fortunately, Benoît came in with great excitement because the tooth fairy had visited during the night. He placed his piggy bank on the table and asked his father to help him unscrew it so he could count his fortune. I watched them do it and told myself that if Vincent's head were a porcelain pig's, I would have shaken and opened it, to finally discover exactly what was inside.

YOU LEFT THE HOSPITAL FIFTEEN DAYS AGO. There's still no question yet of your moving into your new apartment. You're at your parents' in a Manhattan suburb. I've planned to come for the weekend. Despite your mother's insistence, I've turned down her invitation to stay and sleep there. No matter how much she explained to me that I wouldn't find anywhere better to spend the night than a motel on the expressway, I stuck to my guns. You know how much I detest sleeping at anybody's place. I'd rather have the solitude of a room with regulation decor and doubtful hygiene than the unpleasantness of a night spent in someone's home. Whether I know them intimately or not at all doesn't change anything. I'm always afraid I'll damage something. I don't dare go to the bathroom in the middle of the night, and I can't sneak away to the kitchen if I can't sleep. I never know what time one is expected to get up. Finally, why show them the most personal thing about me, the way I look when I'm just out of bed?

We've had this discussion a hundred times. In the beginning, it irritated you; but you ended up understanding my arguments. You even invented a saying intended for me and had it stamped into a wooden ruler that sits prominently on my desk: FRIENDS FOREVER, IN THE DAY BUT NOT AT NIGHT. It's one of my rare principles, but it's an inflexible one.

It's clear you haven't had the time to explain it to your mother.

I haven't spoken to you since my visit to your bedside. That was four months ago. You sent me a few emails. In the end, you've had to ask someone to write them for you. Messages that were warm but that didn't reveal much, and which didn't tell me how you're really doing. The very last email I received was from your father. He was informing me of the exact route for getting from the airport to your place, but he made no mention of your mental condition. He mentions "tenuous but continual progress." There's an embargo on your state of mind. It makes me that much more in a hurry to come and see you.

Hauppauge is an ordinary suburb like the ones I've seen so many times in films. As a result, when I travel to the United States, I always have the feeling that I recognize a place, even one I'm visiting for the first time. It's a wide, peaceful avenue lined with houses that all look alike, with a corner garage on the right, a basketball hoop on the left and a small, well-kept backyard. The weather is mild on this Saturday morning in June. The windows are open, and several cars with gaping doors are being meticulously cared for by an exclusively male population.

In front of your place, the Volvo station wagon has been parked in a hurry. The lawn hasn't been mowed, and the windows are closed. On such a beautiful morning, your parents' house seems to have withdrawn into itself.

A thick wooden board has been placed over the entire width of the stairs leading to the door.

I don't have time to draw any conclusions before the door opens on your mother's ample

figure, belted tightly into a royal-blue tracksuit.
Your father has left on an emergency call to treat
a neighbor's toothache, but she is *so happy* I've
come; and I can tell her enthusiasm is genuine.
With palpable emotion, she takes me in her arms
and whispers in my ear that you're in such a hurry
to see me that she's almost jealous of it, something that makes her laugh but causes me to feel
uncomfortable.

As she hugs me and I drown in billows of her
heady perfume, I catch a glimpse at the entrance
to the living room of the object I hadn't yet
thought of.

Your wheelchair.

Blocking the entrance is this contraption with
wheels in silvered steel and a black-leather back.

Dora has followed my eyes and points at the
immaculate beige floor of her living room with a
tragic expression. "I know. And to think that I just
changed the carpeting! What bad luck. It leaves
horrible marks. I don't know how to get them out."

"Come on in! The popcorn is still a little
warm." You're lying against three thick pillows
in a bed cluttered with magazines, bags of candy,
chips, boxes of chocolate. Your right hand, which

had been buried in the greasy paper bag set in front of your eyes, takes hold of the remote, which you hold toward the screen to mute the sound, but not the image. You're wearing a violet cotton turtleneck that goes all the way up to your chin. Your hair has grown back a bit, but far from its usual length. Your body is engulfed in a thick flowered quilt of some synthetic material whose wrinkle-free surface must please your mother. There's no question about the fact that you're better. Your eyes are more animated, their color clearer (you obviously haven't started smoking again). Your cheeks are rounder as well, the result of all those snacks, which you push aside to make room for me next to you. "Come and lie down next to me. Welcome to Molly's Ark."

You look a little like a rag doll. All of your movements occur in slow motion. But you speak clearly, in your trademark sarcastic tone. That huskiness has finally returned to your voice, even if it still sounds weak and cottony, as if you're out of breath. I'm relieved to see that your expression no longer looks like you've come back from the dead. But I see no spark in your eyes. Only the weight of an indescribable fatigue.

I've picked up a pillow and set my head down against yours. Both of us close our eyes at the same time. I've found you again, at last. You kiss me on the cheek and let out a sigh.

"Look where we are. Do you realize I left this room seventeen years ago, planning never to come back? Which just goes to show, you should never say never." You gesture toward the paper bag. "Have some. I asked for salty, your favorite." I dip my hand into the popcorn. Your eyes follow mine. You smile sadly. "See, I speak a lot better. But that's all. I don't move any better."

There. It's been said. By you, of course, in your way of letting the cat out of the bag, to get a rise out of me.

Just don't react. I shrug. "Sure, for the time being."

You don't answer. I straighten up. You look up at the ceiling, your features closed. "It's not going to come back. And neither will the life that goes along with it."

Tears come from my eyes without my being able to hold them back. They're flowing in silence. You point the remote at the screen again and put the sound back on. Children's voices are singing the praises of a honey-and-caramel-flavored cereal. You take another handful of popcorn and point at the screen: "He's cute, looks like Benoît. He must be about that size, right? What about Clara? Does she still look like you? Got any photos? How old are they now?"

I blow my nose, pick up my phone. I tell you their ages, show you our vacation shots and others taken at their last birthdays. I try to tell some stories and you pretend interest. You ask for news of Vincent, and I avoid the issue by saying he's working too much. I tell you about the renovations being made in our summer house, the surprise I'm planning for my parents' anniversary. You interrupt suddenly: "How old is Clara?" The question throws me because I told you that five minutes ago. On the other hand, you remember perfectly the year you gave her the stuffed kangaroo. You ask me if I know the singer whose video is playing on the screen. It's a sweet song about love and childhood, and you're humming along, but halfheartedly. Suddenly you turn on your right side, shutting your eyes. "I'm going to rest before lunch." By the time I leave the room you're asleep.

On the first floor is a very tall man, a bit stooped, busy in the living room with some bottles on a wheeled table. "Molly told me you liked your tomato juice very spicy. I've put some vodka in mine, should I do the same for yours?" I've seen photos of your father, but I never realized the extent to which he was a reference point for you. I think everyone you've been in love with is this same type: tall, lean, and dark.

Your father studies me with his head tilted slightly to one side, as I've always seen you do when you're concentrating. "You see, Molly remembers the kind of drinks you like, but she asked what day you were coming three times today. She has all her wits about her, but her short-term memory could be a lot better. Supposedly that can still be fixed." He hands me my glass. "I'm not counting on the rest any more." His voice is trembling a bit, as is his hand, and he pours another glass before going on, indicating the wheelchair. "That thing's there for good. You can imagine all the consequences that entails."

Suddenly he raises his voice to call toward the kitchen, where a spoon has just fallen. "You need some help, sweetie?" He waits for an answer, which doesn't come, and goes back to what he was saying. "Her mother doesn't want to hear it, but Molly has adapted to it. Too quickly, in my opinion. The physiotherapist said that to me, too. She isn't giving her all. And I don't understand why. I know there's not much chance she'll recover, but they've already seen miracles with patients who refuse to consider their life in a wheelchair. They put everything they've got into trying and get results that go beyond all expectations." He leans closer to me. "Do you understand why she's given up so quickly?"

The sound of a small bell makes him leap to his feet on his long legs, and he sets his glass down. "Ah! My princess wants to come downstairs! I'm going to get her."

I'm seated facing you. You're propped up as best you can in your wheelchair by two cushions that are too limp. Lunch for you is carrot juice that you drink with a straw, some poached whitefish, and mashed potatoes. You mix all of it with a spoon, and the effort it takes you to eat is heartbreaking. You don't make any attempt to wipe away the liquid trickling from the corner of your lips, and your parents pay no attention to it. At one moment you bang your cheek a little against your spoon without reacting. Obviously. That side of your face doesn't feel anything. The liquid flows along your jaw beyond the edge of your turtleneck. I'm watching a clumsy, helpless little girl. You smile lovingly at me, despite the fact that I can't manage to look at your face and your lifeless mouth. My Molly. My stomach is in knots. I ask blankly where the bathroom is and leave for the end of the hallway to shut myself up in it. For weeks I've been imagining you like a patient in a novel, languishing in a comfortable armchair with a shawl over your knees, sitting near a window and listening to music or busy writing on your laptop, your back straight against the pillows, your eyes looking lively beneath your long hair — but not these sagging shoulders, this face too heavy for your neck, this drained, snuffed-out expression.

We spend the afternoon in your room, whose curtains I've closed to keep it cool. I think both of us fell asleep in front of the television, lulled by the music of a channel showing music videos. Around five o'clock your mother brings up two bowls of ice cream for us. We watch a US Open tennis match. I suggest we put on TCM, the channel devoted to the old films you used to love, but you explain that you don't succeed in concentrating long enough to follow a story any more. There's the hint of a smile on your face as you nudge me with your elbow. "You'll like this: I can't even finish an article in *People* magazine." I burst out laughing. That dig is the old Molly coming to the surface. You lower the sound of the TV. "You know what? Nothing interests me. For weeks I've been sleeping. I don't think of anything, and I especially don't want to mull over things."

You turn your face toward mine, and for the first time since I arrived, I sense you're about to break down. "You used to say I was a softie and a chicken? Well, you were right. I don't even have the nerve to end it all. I could, you know. The drawer is full of drugs. But nope. I'd rather spend the rest of my life channel surfing in bed. That'll be some rest, right?" Tears are forming at the corners of your eyes. "Somebody up there must have played heads or tails, and it ended up falling on me."

I take you in my arms, rock you gently. "Go ahead and cry, my Molly, let it out, it will do you good. Don't forget that they're stuffing you with tranquilizers, sedatives. You've got to let some time pass." I'm murmuring those hollow remarks you resort to when you've run out of arguments. You don't let yourself be consoled for very long. You sit up to blow your nose, then fall back on the pillows that I've just straightened. You go back to your TV zapping and watch the channels go by.

"You don't understand. It's too hard. I'm about to turn forty-one. Who am I supposed to be fighting for? For the guy I don't have? For the children I'll never have? I'm tired. Could you tell my mother I'd like to have dinner?"

As I'm getting up, the door opens on the nurse, a young perky blond woman in her thirties with a sparkling smile, who sticks a needle in the vein on your right arm without ever stopping her talking. "And how are we today? We've got a visitor from France? Oh, but we must be a *very important person* for somebody to come see us from as far away as that! Ah, Paris! Chanel! I've always dreamed about it . . ." Normally, that kind of creature would have aggravated you and we would have made fun of her together; but in this situation she seems to be a distraction. She's even soothing, unless it's the immediate effect of the intravenous injection.

Your mother serves you dinner at six thirty: a bowl of consommé and a plate of pasta that you eat in your bed while we watch the top twenty music videos of the week. "You see, they last around two and a half minutes, the ideal length for my brain. I think it shrank during my coma. It certainly is the only part of my body that lost weight, right? Are you sure you don't want to stay and sleep over?" I should have said yes. It was easy to tell that it would have given you pleasure. I explain to you that your father has already dropped off my bag at the motel, a lousy excuse since it's five minutes away and I could easily go back and get it. But I absolutely need to get out of that room with its pink wallpaper and immaculate carpeting — out of this house in mourning, away from this inconsolable suffering.

It's Sunday, and the weather is even more beautiful than yesterday. Dora has called me early to tell me that you're going to come and get me by car, that you feel like getting some air. I went to get you a bouquet of flowers at the supermarket on the corner, and I'm waiting for you at the side of the road, my face in the sun. You're sitting in the back of the Volvo in a gray, shapeless sweatshirt, and it enrages me to see you forgo your usual interest in your appearance. You look like you're in a good mood, and you smell the peonies as if you were going to bite into them. I'm thrilled that my being here has made you want to go out.

When the car enters a giant parking lot, I understand my mistake. I'd forgotten that the expression *go out for a walk* means ambling through a shopping mall where you can do everything: eat Italian or Japanese, buy candy or a TV set, go to the cosmetician or a hairdressing salon, or fill a shopping cart while your ears are drowned in the voices of the latest hit singers. What could be more depressing than moving through aisles turned freezing by air-conditioning while pushing your wheelchair?

But you seem happy to see some people, to feel yourself in a familiar world, designed so that a wheelchair can roll absolutely everywhere, from the parking lot elevator to the restrooms of the restaurant. You do seem livelier this morning. You make caustic remarks about ill-mannered children who yell without their parents objecting. You're interested in the shop windows. You buy a new eau de toilette, let me get you a silk scarf in a blend of blues that soften your coloring. Impulsively you let yourself be made up at a stand and leave with a kit containing an array of products. We stop to admire an exhibition of black-and-white photos. You smell nachos very near, and you want some. We head for the Mexican restaurant nearby, where you enjoy a bowl of guacamole and a chocolate ice cream.

We're waiting for the check when a pretty, very pregnant brunette breaks away from the group passing in front of our table and stops there as she lets out a shout. "Molly, is it you? I don't believe it. It's me, Lisa! Do you recognize me? We studied ballet together in grade school!" Suddenly she stops and turns red. She's just noticed the wheelchair. Molly gives her a faint smile. "I remember very well. But I'm not sure that a tutu's still right for me." The arrival of the waitress gives poor Lisa a chance to slip away.

Dora decides that we shouldn't linger because of traffic holdups, and you allow yourself to be pushed to the car without saying a word. The way back passes in a silence that the country music station isn't enough to make up for. When your father helps you back into your bed, it's already four p.m. I can't stay any longer or I'll miss my flight. I bend over the flowered comforter and hold you against me with all my strength. I don't want to stay, but I'm in despair at the prospect of leaving you. I feel as if I'm abandoning you, letting you down. From your gray sweatshirt you take out a yellow sheet of paper folded in fourths, with my name on it. "Here, this is my new motto. Promise me you'll think of me every day." I promise, choking back tears, kiss you as if I'll never see you again. I've never left anyone with such a feeling of defeat, futility.

I wait for the taxi to turn the corner of the street before I unfold your message. It's scathing, appalling.

Enjoy while it lasts. It doesn't.

YOU SPENT THE SUMMER AT YOUR PARENTS'. Then, in the fall, things had to be organized; in other words, what your life was going to become had to be put into place. That beautiful apartment with its terrace and its southern exposure near Columbus Avenue, where you were planning on spending, as you would put it, "a life with a view," was reimagined with the functioning of the wheelchair in mind. You can no longer live alone. At night, in the day, during the week and weekend, nurses, massage therapists, and home health aides take their shifts assisting you.

You don't describe your day-to-day life in the rare emails you send me. Your messages are typed text-style, something you detested. To me they seem terse, loving, sad.

You ask me to tell you about my life, but that's exactly what I now have trouble doing. At every moment, as I run down the street, climb stairs, go to the gym, or simply when I'm taking a walk, having a coffee at a counter, going downstairs to buy a magazine, or when I'm cooking, putting the children to bed, I tell myself that I'm doing all these daily, banal things without a thought, whereas you will never be able to do them again; and I want to scream with helplessness and shame. Shame at having a normal life while yours has ceased to be one. Shame at having had luck. Shame at feeling alive. I'm afraid that the slightest anecdote I could share with you would only end up wounding you more, that in reading me you sense the extent to which I'm taking advantage of each second of my life, whereas you no longer have the freedom to lead yours. Suddenly I'm confining myself to banalities that say nothing about me but that at least can't cause you pain. I search for a breezy, enthusiastic tone, but it's easy for me to see that my emails are getting further apart and shorter, more impersonal, summary.

You must think that I'm forgetting you, but I think of you nonstop.

You must be imagining that I have nothing to tell you, but I need to talk to you so much . . .

You must think that my life is sweet, full of joy, and that my marriage is fulfilling, but three words on a cell phone have turned me into this tense, nervous, unhappy woman I scarcely recognize.

I still haven't spoken to Vincent. I can't do it.

As long as the words aren't spoken, the things they conceal have no reality. I can't say the words *lover*, *mistress*, *affair* out loud. They would dirty us. I'd be too afraid that they'd become irrevocable.

And then there's the question of pride, too.

Not us. Not that. We're worth more than that, after all.

Molly, you would have been proud of me.

This Friday, the children were with my parents for the weekend. We were going out to the movies. Vincent and I. We were at the door, putting on our coats. Suddenly I noticed that he was feeling his pockets, looking around. I knew what he was searching for. A little earlier, I'd seen him put his newspaper on top of his cell phone.

I couldn't keep from saying something.

Why couldn't I?

I pushed aside the newspaper, grabbed the phone, and held it out to him, saying, "I know what's in your cell phone."

He put it in his pocket without saying anything, as if he hadn't heard or understood, as if he could afford to ignore something that didn't make any sense.

I insisted, didn't move. "The messages. The girl who misses you."

In a few seconds, his expression changed from surprise to incomprehension, and then ended with a touch of disdainfulness. I could see on his face that he was thinking very quickly, looking for the best way to respond, the best option possible.

Molly, this is terrible to say, but I swear to you: for the first time in twenty years of life together, Vincent looked like a moron. Like an imbecile.

With a smile that was hoping to put an end to it but that only looked inane, he said, "Messages are private."

"It rang while you were taking a nap."

Nothing. Three seconds of silence. An eternity.

I went back on the attack: "So?"

He stuck his hands in his pockets, took out his keys. "So . . . It's my private business."

"That private business is now out."

He spread apart his arms, his expression contrite. A kid caught with his fingers in the cookie jar. "Listen . . . She's young, from the sticks, she's a little lost . . . I was giving her some advice. She's easy to impress." He took my arm, brought his face close to mine, and finally looked me in the eye. "It's nothing at all, OK? Would you trust me? Now, can we go?"

He spent the movie holding my hand like a schoolboy trying to kiss a girl in the dark for the first time. I don't remember a thing about the film. I felt frozen. I wanted to throw up, scream, bite. I wanted to go back to the house. But was our home still mine?

IT WILL BE A YEAR SINCE YOU COLLAPSED ALONG YOUR PLATE GLASS WINDOW, and the profession, which adores anniversaries, has chosen to honor you. Nothing glitzy, no formal wear, nothing for the paparazzi to go crazy about. But nonetheless: I've been invited to an evening in your honor, which, as the embossed invitation in gold letters says, will "celebrate her invaluable contribution to the domain of cinema."

Immediately I had my doubts. It was too soon after your accident. I hardly dared imagine your reaction.

I was wrong, which I learned while speaking to you over the phone. You are delighted, as thrilled as a little girl who was dreaming of having a Barbie doll and has suddenly learned that she has won the entire toy store. Since that time, every three days you've sent me the updated list of the growing number of people who've agreed to speak. You seem sincerely proud and touched by this sign of consideration.

At first I warned you that it would be impossible for me to attend the festivities because months earlier I'd already accepted being part of a jury at a festival in the provinces. Finally, I took advantage of the festival having changed its dates by withdrawing from the jury. I didn't tell you that. I can't wait to see your expression that night when you see me in the room.

I let Tom in on it, wrote the most beautiful congratulatory speech I could think of and learned it by heart, put a pair of black trousers and some heels in my suitcase. I'm thrilled to be in the Hamptons, that stretch of sea two hours from Manhattan where fashionable New Yorkers love to vacation, on an island that has been immortalized by Fitzgerald in his novel. Tom has explained to me that you have to know the difference between Southampton, which borders on old money, private incomes, writers, from East Hampton, which has become the preserve of the trendy and the nouveaux riches, such as traders, actors, and producers. Those are the people who created that weekend minifestival each year when a figure from the world of film is celebrated with an "industry toast." It's the kind of evening where respected professionals come to give speeches in honor of one of their own, during which they must appear humble, mischievous, scathing, moving, generous, and a good buddy — all within ten minutes.

The Maidstone Hotel is one of those delightfully refined places where you need to make reservations for a weekend a year in advance. My room is hung with striped beige wallpaper of very much the latest fashion. It smells like rosewood, and I hope, Molly, that your bed is covered with the same gigantic soft eiderdown on which I definitely cannot lie as I'm afraid I'll fall right to sleep. I alternate Coca-Colas with espressos shut up in my room, for fear of running into someone close to you.

Around six p.m. Tom comes to get me and take me to the grand salon, a room with wooden wainscoted walls, where about sixty guests are distributed around ten round tables. On the stage, a video screen and a mike are waiting for the participants. A best-of-Tina-Turner selection of songs intended for you blares through old loudspeakers with a badly adjusted equalizer so that the bass makes the stemmed glasses tremble on the white tablecloths.

I'm standing at your table, waiting for you. I have checked out the names. You'll be seated with Peter, Paul, Tom, and some other colleagues, no one but people from the film world. Maybe this evening will inspire you to take up your former occupation again? I know that for now you're leafing through screenplays without reading them, that you aren't watching the DVDs they send your way, that you're only interested in box office results and evenings at the Oscars. That saddens Tom and anguishes me.

The room is almost full. The men are in dark suits, the women in cocktail dresses. For once, I'm grateful for the slightly provincial formalism of the Americans. In Paris for this kind of evening, the men would have dispensed with ties and the women would be in jeans. Here, everyone has made an effort to look elegant in your honor. I recognize most of the faces. The majority of your list responded to the invitation. Suddenly I'm conscious of the value of their presence. This really is an example of your peers paying homage to you. I can feel a lump forming in my throat.

Tina Turner has disappeared from the amps. Peter and Paul are taking hold of the mike under the applause and are warming the room up. "Thank you for interrupting your work and weekend to be here on this last Friday in October. All of you know and appreciate the person whom we are about to celebrate. For us she's more essential than the sun, the moon, and the stars. It's for her that we're here this evening. Ladies and gentlemen, let's all warmly welcome Miss Molly B!"

The two leaves of the door open on the wheels of your chair. You're wearing a gold lamé jacket and black slacks, a bit too much lipstick, which hardens your face, and some eye shadow that is too dark. There are blond streaks in your hair, which looks good on you. Your father pushes you to the center of the room, right opposite the onstage mike. In close-up I can see your frightened eyes and half smile.

The speeches follow upon one another, and with them, the memories. They celebrate your intuition, your loyalty, your business sense.

Almodóvar has even recorded a video message explaining why he loves working with you. The trailers for the films you've bought begin playing. Most of them we acquired together. Regularly, your face caught on-screen by a video camera is replaced by photos. That alternation between your former face and the one you have this evening is almost too cruel for me to handle. When it's my turn to speak, I've completely forgotten my well-phrased congratulatory speech. I know only one thing: since the others have spoken of the past, I'm going to speak about you in the present. I take hold of the mike as if I was going to sing the blues, and I improvise, for you, as I look into your eyes:

"Molly, you are one of the people who mean the most to me, but as someone who loves ranking, you'll be sorry to find out that you're only in fourth place in my personal life. The winning position has been taken by force by my husband, Clara, and Benoît. Sorry . . ." The laughter in the room has warmth. You smile at me. You don't even seem surprised by my presence. I lean toward you. "Molly, you perform this profession with passion and discipline. You're better informed than your competitors. Is it because you get up earlier, or because you go to bed later? I have followed you wherever you went for years to learn your secret, and I think I've discovered it. It's in your heart that it happens. You put more heart into it than all of us. The same goes for friendship. You put more heart into it than the others. That is why I'm proud to be in your life, to be your friend. Long live Molly!"

It's dreadfully banal and facile, but the Americans adore grand words like *heart*, *friendship*, *secret*. I go back to my seat to the sound of applause. I'm not proud of myself. I would have liked to speak to you more subtly, with more panache and style. But what does it matter, since you look happy. I drink a large glass of water. The people at my table congratulate me. The evening goes on.

An hour later, we've finished our appetizers and the main dish has just been served, but the tributes are still sounding from the stage. The heat is becoming stifling. The headwaiters perform their tasks while ignoring the speeches and toasts presented with forced enthusiasm by the participants, into a mike that is sending whistling noises into the amps. I can sense that the evening, which began with a feeling of breeziness and warmth, is starting to flag. Your wheelchair has been pushed to our table. Now you're at my side. You don't eat anything. You confided in me that you'd had dinner before so that no one would see you struggling with your utensils. There's no straw in the champagne glass that you pretend to drink from. You're also faking your smiles. These tributes are like so many stabs of a dagger. All they are doing is reminding you of what will never again be. This gathering resembles a perfectly organized wedding to which they had merely forgotten to invite the betrothed. There is no reason to rejoice, nothing to celebrate, no hope on the horizon. The bride is in black, and this celebration is turning into a first-class funeral. That of your brilliant career.

Before dessert is served, the wire to the mike is pulled from the stage so that you can take hold of it without having to move. This is your moment to return the compliments. A small piece of paper has been placed in front of you by your father, who has taken it from his bag. It contains the list of all those you'd like to thank, something you do with grace and sweetness, with a word for each.

Your throaty voice is still a bit frail, and the emotion makes it tremble. All of a sudden, everyone has stopped eating, and the silence in which we are all listening is our most beautiful sign of respect. My name is not on your sheet of paper, but you thank me for having come and, as I did, improvise, turning to look at me.

"You thought you were going to surprise me this evening, but I knew you'd find a way to come. Besides, your perfume gave you away. I smelled it in the hotel lobby, my French friend. In your country, the flag is blue like the way you love to eat steaks, white like the movie screen before the film begins, and red like the heart of our friendship that will never stop beating."

I hide my face in my napkin. It's the most beautiful thing you've ever said to me. Then you put down your paper and raise your glass of champagne, which is nearly full. "I thank all of you for coming. I loved this evening, as I have loved every second I have spent in your company. Soon we'll leave one another. I'll let you run all over the world, in the whirlwind of your work. As for me, all my life I've dreamed of taking an early retirement to go and live in Tuscany. This evening, as you can see, I've already carried out the first part of my program."

As if he'd waited for the end of your sentence to rush forward, a waiter comes toward you, trips on the microphone wire, and overturns his tray loaded with crèmes brûlées at your feet. God bless him. The overall hilarity his fall provokes keeps us from bursting into tears.

You signal your father, pointing out the door toward the restroom, but you also whisper in my ear as you place your right hand on mine, "This is too much emotion for me. I'm going to slip away without saying goodbye. What I said is true: I was sure you would come. The bit about the flag — I was thinking about it for three days. Not bad, huh?"

Since you have left, and because Peter, Paul, and Tom are going back to New York this evening, I decide to have a last drink at the hotel bar with Suzie. She lives a few blocks from your new apartment. She must be best able to tell me how you're coping from day to day.

I would have done better to go to bed early. According to her, you've become "difficult." The word makes my blood boil. Who in your place, condemned from one day to the next to go from hyperactivity to humiliating immobility, wouldn't become like that? You, difficult? Instead, I find you defeated, apathetic, resigned. Suzie doesn't at all agree. She gives me a portrait of you devoid of kindness. "Molly has changed a lot, and really not in a good way. It's as if the world owes her a living, and everybody has to bow to her needs. For example, she'll arrange to be with you and then cancel at the last minute without excuses. Or else when you've taken the time to come and see her, she'll get rid of you just like that, without even offering you a glass of water, just because she feels tired. She doesn't make any effort, leaves her TV on all the time, and watches it out of the corner of her eye even when you're with her. You can imagine how much fun that is. No, I can assure you, she expects a lot of other people, with the excuse that she's housebound . . ."

I'm shocked to discover that your American friends are slowly but surely dropping you. They're sick of your demands, which always include the need for some favor from them. They find your humor more and more wounding, your company less and less pleasant. They think you've become rather stingy and that you're always talking about money.

Tom, whom I call the next day from the airport to tell him about this conversation, tries to soften the portrait, but does admit that you can sometimes be difficult. "She's not always perfectly nice, you know."

I don't get over my anger during the entire trip back. And why should you be nice? Illness doesn't make people better. Living in a wheelchair hasn't transformed you into Mother Teresa. And I'm glad it hasn't. You're still the same, probably more acidic, more brutal, more curt, more radical, more impatient, more intransigent. I understand you. Now that you know you're condemned to passivity, you're fighting with the only weapon left to you: your brain power.

IT'S THE BEGINNING OF MARCH, AND NEW YORK IS ALREADY HAVING MILD SPRING WEATHER. This time you've told me to come to your place. The building is welcoming with its silver canopy on the outside and its thick blue carpeting, as is proper for homes in the nicer neighborhoods.

The uniformed doorman bows as he opens the glass door for me; with the same gesture and without ever being discourteous, he inquires about my identity and goes to check the register to see if I'm really expected, then smiles and finally looks me in the eye. "I see, you're the French woman? I'm Mr. Dennis. Let me welcome you." He walks ahead of me to the elevator, pushes open the heavy iron door, and presses the button for your floor, as if he were receiving me in his own home.

The heat that pervades the apartment attacks my throat as soon as the door opens on a stout young black woman squeezed into a white T-shirt and sparkly red tracksuit. She shakes my hand without warmth before leading me behind her softly undulating backside to the living room, where she announces me in too loud a voice. "Molly, your friend is here." She turns to me and adds incredulously, "Did you really come *all the way* from Paris? *I love French men, they're gorgeous!*" Exploding into laughter, she plants herself right there with crossed arms while you kiss me, moved as we are to see each other again, and while I whisper a few tender words into your ear. She ends up interrupting us. "I'm Dinah, want something to drink?"

I'm dying for a nice cold Coke, but I tell myself that tea will take the longest to prepare. She goes to work in another room, from which she emerges less than two minutes later with a tray on which she's hurriedly placed a kettle that is barely warm, a cup, and a tea bag. She puts all of it on a low table without taking the time to push aside a pile of magazines. She joins us quite peremptorily, standing there, her arms crossed, back leaning against a shelf. I know how much you love to steep your smoked Lapsang Souchong in a red stoneware teapot that you brought back from Paris, and I wait for you to reproach her for her offhand way of throwing together my tea, but you say nothing. You seem resigned, or else you're too tired to notice anything at all. Dinah's presence doesn't seem to weigh on you, any more than the sound of the television whose volume I end up lowering with the remote, although I don't dare turn it off completely. You seem happy to see me, and as usual you ask me a thousand questions about the children, my parents, our friends in common; but you still seem to have trouble concentrating on my answers. Your voice sounds steadier to me this morning than it did that evening in the Hamptons, but your eyes look more extinguished.

At any rate, it's so warm that my head starts spinning, and I'm sure you're suffering from it as well. I suggest we open the glass door leading to the terrace. "She's going to expose us to a draft," comments Dinah in a reproving tone. "She made me catch cold less than two weeks ago."

That way of talking about you as if you weren't there immediately irks me. "You know, fresh air gets rid of germs," I say in a decisive tone.

It makes you smile. "I see you've kept your fighting spirit, unlike me."

I take hold of your chair and push it onto the terrace, nimbly shutting the door before Dinah has the time to venture outside with us.

I let out a loud sigh. "Say, does she stick to you that much all the time?"

You merely lift your eyebrows. "It's complicated, you know. Dad has a lot of trouble finding honest girls!" You start to tell me a sleazy tale of the previous nurse stealing a wallet. You admit that you suspect the one before her had a copy of your keys made; and besides that, you recently had the door to your apartment reinforced, which seemed way too expensive to you. "The worst are on the weekends, when three girls take turns. But you know, it's kind of them to spend their time with me. I wouldn't have that job for all the money in the world."

I roll my eyes. "Sure, Molly, OK, but you don't have their brain, either."

Sadly, you gaze off into the distance. "You know, if you have to live in a wheelchair all day, it's better to be mindless and think of nothing. I'm practicing, see, I live with the television on all day, that'll make my gray matter go to pot, don't you think?"

No, I don't think so, but your sadness breaks my heart.

You point toward Dinah with your chin. "You know, I like the two of us alone together more, but I think it would entertain her having company, too. I'm so shitty to live with that I really owe her that."

I tell myself that I'm going to have a hard time resisting your gloominess and that a change in mood is vital. I suggest improvising a lunch on your terrace.

Your face lights up and comes to life immediately. "We can go to the Italian supermarket, they've got some delicious products. I've been dreaming of your mozzarella and tomatoes. Remember you made some for me in Paris? Dinah will go with us because I've totally lost my sense of direction."

I help Dinah move you to another wheelchair, one that can be folded, less comfortable but better adapted to the size of the elevator. It takes us a good five minutes, and already you've gone pale and are winded. I go to get you a glass of water. You drink it in one gulp. You close your eyes. There. You're breathing better.

Now we've got to get your coat on, your scarf. The idea of coming out of your cocoon has you flushed and sweating. Dinah, who is obviously used to it, is caressing your hand. She begins listing things you'd better buy. Then you decide that the list should be written down, because you are afraid we'll forget something. I look for a piece of paper, a pen. Your anxiety is at such a level that Dinah has to open her purse twice to show you that she really has remembered the keys and the wallet. You send her to get another shopping basket, because you think the one she is carrying won't be enough. All of this takes about twenty minutes.

When the elevator arrives, I see immediately that it's too small for the three of us, but before I have the time to offer to go down on foot, Dinah is ahead of me. "Could you go down and tell Dennis to help us? The downstairs door is so heavy." As I rush down the stairs, I tell myself that I have judged Dinah a little too quickly. Yes, she's intrusive, but she knows what she's doing; and I see what a delicate operation it is to take care of you the right way.

The air on Columbus Avenue is mild. Dinah pushes the wheelchair and I make conversation. But I can tell that you're distracted, anxious. You tensed up as soon as we had to cross the street. And then, everything frightens you. A dog barking, a child crying, a car horn, a police siren. When I point out to you how pleasant the sun on your face is, and ask Dinah to stop for a moment so that you can enjoy it a little, enjoy that sun that you so worshipped before, you shut your eyes and start breathing in tiny little gasps, as if you had to take precautions with everything, even with harmless things that are supposed to do you good, like taking advantage of a moment of nice weather.

It's impossible not to be aware of the nationality of the products being sold in the small market we've just entered. As we go in, there are blinking neon lights in the colors of the Italian flag. From the loudspeakers come Neapolitan arias. The manager behind the cash register looks like a Soprano from the suburbs.

"Wait'll you see," you tell me, suddenly excited, "their *burrata* is out of this world!"

Dinah gets her two cents in immediately. "But it's much too expensive! The price of the mozzarella is so much more reasonable. Especially since it's just to put a few little pieces in a tomato salad."

Gently but firmly, I explain to Dinah that today it's my treat, because I'm the one who's going to prepare the food. You move on by asking her in a conciliatory tone if she wouldn't mind taking care of the rest of the list, because she'll do it a lot more quickly than will I, who doesn't know how the food is arranged, and while she does, you and I can go and pick out the lunch food. We agree to meet at the checkout. Dinah is sullen about it, but can only comply.

I use the situation to take everything back in hand: you, your wheelchair, and the spirit of doing the errands. I have you smell cheeses that you aren't familiar with, sample several kinds of sausages, discover the sesame crackers I adore and the *grissini* dipped in chocolate that Clara and Benoît are crazy about. I choose a good wine and pick a bouquet of basil. To my great satisfaction, you're smiling again and your color has come back. Just before we get to the checkout, you stretch out your right arm toward a shelf. "Did you see, they have the best pasta, the blue box. Dinah never wants to buy it, she thinks it costs too much, but why not get just one pack and say you're the one who had the idea? If not, she'll be furious." I'm distracted by the line in front of the cash register and listening to you with one ear. I don't quite understand what you're saying, and I don't see what the problem is with this pasta, which truly is supposed to be the best. In any case, it's your money Dinah's spending and you should get what you want. Suddenly, this gets on my nerves, and I take two packs of it, with two cans of a sauce that seems appetizing.

At the cash register, Dinah is watching me put down what I'm buying. She goes straight for the blue packets as soon as they appear on the moving belt and promptly removes them. "Oh no, Molly! We said that was too expensive." Contrite, you lower your eyes without daring to respond.

Outraged, I keep control of myself to remain polite. "Leave it, Dinah. Today I'm paying," I say firmly.

Dinah turns toward me, looks me in the eye, then looks me up and down. "Fine. Since that's the way it is, there's no need for me anymore. I'll leave you alone." She bends toward us, puts back the packets, and, with a theatrical gesture, leaves behind the keys and the basket on your knees. Then she turns and heads for the door.

Your shriek, Molly, is engraved forever in my memory. A child being torn away from his family wouldn't have screamed as violently.

The Neapolitan singers seem to have doubled in volume, in this luxury minisupermarket where everyone has suddenly become silent.

Dinah continues imperturbably to amble toward the exit.

Finally, she stops at the threshold of the door and gives herself five long seconds of pure melodrama before coming back.

This time, I'm the one she's heading for. "See? She absolutely cannot get so worked up."

Finally, she decides to place her two hands on the back of your wheelchair. She looks at me triumphantly, bends toward you, takes out a pack of tissues, and delicately wipes a strand of drool that has flowed from your mouth. Then she produces a small bottle of mineral water from her bag and has you drink through a straw while caressing your hair.

We leave the store, attempting to save face as much as possible. The blue packets have stayed behind on the moving belt.

You'll pretend to doze all the way back.

Dinah remained for six more months. After her there was Sally, then Nancy. Right now it's Eva, a Puerto Rican. I don't know where they come from, whether they're from an agency. I'm unaware whether it's your father who still chooses them. It really doesn't matter. They're all built from the same model: patient, calm, available. Incredible girls. Lalas for adults who, inevitably, end up assuming the power. Depending on the personality of each, the blackmail takes different forms but remains the same. Life is a jungle. And you, my Molly, are now like Babar in the big city. You've lost your defenses.

I NEVER DID FIND OUT WHAT HAD REALLY HAPPENED WITH THE YOUNG STUDENT. Vincent's cell phone once again lies around anywhere at all without him worrying about it.

He barely remembers to recharge it.

We've never spoken about that episode again.

For the first time in my life, I gave up.

Instead of taking it all the way and doing battle, I let it slide.

Out of wisdom or cowardice?

I keep the marks of it inside me.

An indelible, painful, humiliating scar.

Jealousy.

I hated it.

You're still living in the same apartment. You never went back to work.

Films interest you a lot less than before. At least, that's what you say. I think instead your short-term memory continues to play tricks on you. You're completely refocused on music, and you've got a talent for digging up rhythm-and-blues singers who are as obscure as they are talented. But Tina Turner is still your favorite.

You never forget your friends' birthdays, nor their spouses' or their children's.

The day Tom got married, you ended up admitting to me that if you had had someone like him to love, maybe you would have fought harder.

You're still the most caustic, the most brilliant girl I know.

The most direct, too.

Last week, I told you that I'd spent ten hours in a plane next to a delightful passenger and had only discovered when we arrived that she was in a wheelchair. "There are plenty of people who get along on their own despite their handicap and who travel. Don't you want to come back to Europe, to see Venice and Paris again?" Your answer was cutting: "As long as I can't piss alone, I'm not going anywhere. Get that?"

THE MOLLY TO WHOM I WAS WRITING NO LONGER EXISTS.

However, when I think of you, when I wonder what you'd say, how you'd react to things that I am experiencing without you, you're always the same.

A fighter and a conqueror.

I never think of your wheelchair.

That Molly only materializes when I see you.

When I am with you, in that living room where you have again put up all the photos of your previous life, I become aware that you still can't drink without a straw, that you've gained weight, that the television is always on, that you are hooked on Facebook, Twitter, LinkedIn, and all the social networks, that you can't succeed in concentrating on any book, any DVD, that you sometimes fall asleep in the middle of a sentence.

When I'm with you, I rediscover your devastating repartee, the precision of your memories, the distinctive nature of your intelligence.

I rediscover to a small extent how we are in league.

At the moment of leaving you, I feel your sadness and I try to hide mine from you.

I spend the rest of the day with a lump in my throat.

With all my strength I've wanted our friendship to remain intact.

I've got to face facts: that's far from being the case.

I lack courage.

Molly, I'm admitting it to you.

There have been times when I've been in New York and haven't told you.

MICHÈLE HALBERSTADT is a journalist, author, and producer of such films as *Monsieur Ibrahim*, *Farewell My Concubine*, and *Murderous Maids*, which she also cowrote. Her novels include *La Petite* and *The Pianist in the Dark*, which won the Drouot Literary Prize and was short-listed for the Lilas literary prize in France.

BRUCE BENDERSON is a novelist and essayist as well as a translator. He is the author of a memoir, *The Romanian: Story of an Obsession*, winner of France's prestigious Prix de Flore in French translation, and the novels *User* and *Pacific Agony*.

⚏ OTHER PRESS

You might also enjoy these titles from our list:

LA PETITE by Michèle Halberstadt

La Petite is neither grim nor sentimental. Every woman will recognize something of herself in this moving story about adolescent grief, solitude, and awakening.

"[A] touching glimpse of a young life nearly lost and then redeemed...[A] brief but powerful memoir...A haunting story with a triumphant conclusion." —*Kirkus*

COUPLE MECHANICS by Nelly Alard

At once sexy and feminist, this is a story of a woman who decides to fight for her marriage after her husband confesses to an affair with a notable politician.

"Nelly Alard delves into the core of infidelity with wry observation and subtlety. Riveting, beautifully detailed, and totally addictive. You won't be able to put this down." —Tatiana de Rosnay, *New York Times* best-selling author of *Sarah's Key*

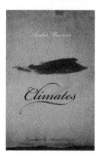

CLIMATES by André Maurois

First published in 1928, this magnificently written novel about a double conjugal failure is imbued with subtle yet profound psychological insights of a caliber that arguably rivals Tolstoy's.

"*Climates* is a delicious romantic bonbon that yanks the heartstrings." —*Wall Street Journal*

Also recommended:

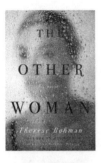

THE OTHER WOMAN by Therese Bohman

A psychological novel where questions of class, status, and ambition loom over a young woman's passionate love affair

"Bohman has a nose for danger: Her characters are curiously, alarmingly awake, and a story we should all know well is transformed into something wondrous and strange. A disturbing, unforgettable book." —Rufi Thorpe, author of *The Girls from Corona del Mar*

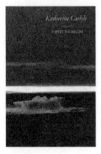

KATHERINE CARLYLE by Rupert Thomson

Unmoored by her mother's death, Katherine Carlyle abandons the set course of her life and starts out on a mysterious journey to the ends of the world.

"The strongest and most original novel I have read in a very long time...It's a masterpiece." —Philip Pullman, author of the best-selling His Dark Materials trilogy

ALL DAYS ARE NIGHT by Peter Stamm

A novel about survival, self-reliance, and art, by Peter Stamm, finalist for the 2013 Man Booker International Prize

"A postmodern riff on *The Magic Mountain*... a page-turner." —*The Atlantic*

"*All Days Are Night* air[s] the psychological implications of our beauty obsession and the insidious ways in which it can obscure selfhood." —*New Republic*

▉ OTHER PRESS

www.otherpress.com